Pride Publishing books by Thom Collins

Jagged Shores

DEEP WATERS

THOM COLLINS

Deep Waters
ISBN # 978-1-80250-504-7
©Copyright Thom Collins 2022
Cover Art by Kelly Martin ©Copyright December 2022
Interior text design by Claire Siemaszkiewicz
Pride Publishing

DEEP WATERS

Dedication

To absent friends, gone but never forgotten.

Chapter One

By late October every year, the tourists left Nyemouth to holiday in the warmer climate of the Mediterranean and the Canary Islands. Making a living wasn't easy in the winter months for the locals who relied on seasonal summer trade. From the start of autumn to the dying days of spring, Harry Renner was grateful for every private charter that came his way. Today was no exception. When the man had called to say he wanted to hire Harry and his boat for two full days of sightseeing, he didn't care why. He took the booking.

Even better, this guy, Christian, wanted to take the boat on Monday and Tuesday. Harry had weekend bookings until the end of November, private fishing parties and afternoon seal-watching trips, but the weekday work was sparse this time of year.

They had spent the morning sailing north. Unlike most of the men who chartered *The North Star*, Christian wasn't interested in fishing. He'd asked

Harry to show him the rugged coastline all the way up to Bamburgh Castle, more fascinated by the shore than any of the birds and wildlife Harry had pointed out. Harry had brought his cousin Tom along to crew the boat, but there had been almost nothing for him to do besides make tea and set out their lunches. All their client seemed interested in was taking photos of the land.

"We might have to put in an hour earlier than planned," Harry shouted from his position in the wheelhouse.

Christian raised his eyes from his camera, a questioning expression on his face.

Harry pointed east at the heavy grey clouds, low on the horizon. "There's bad weather coming." The sky to their shore side was clear, but it wouldn't last. He'd hoped the low-pressure front would hold off until the end of the day, but it looked to be coming faster than expected. If they were lucky, they would have another two hours. That would be enough time to turn the boat around and make it to the shelter of Nyemouth Harbour, but he doubted they had that long. The wind was already picking up, and he guessed things would get lumpy in the next sixty to ninety minutes. "The forecast for tomorrow is a lot better. We can make up for the time we lose today then — if that's all right with you."

Christian gave a curt nod.

He wasn't much of a talker. He'd asked a lot of questions but had little to say for himself. When he'd turned up at the dock that morning, Christian Costner was not what Harry had expected. A lot of the men who booked private charters were of a type...arseholes. They would usually turn up with expensive fishing equipment, often brand new, in designer waterproofs and wearing their Rolex and TAG watches. They invariably brought along an entourage — the beta males to their alpha — guys beneath them they could show off to and lord it over. Harry wasn't proud. If they had money to spend, he would take it — anything to put away for winter. For some reason, that was exactly what he'd expected of this guy.

Christian had turned up alone, which had been the first surprise. He wore jeans, a thick sweater and a regular jacket with no obvious designer label. Harry guessed he was in his early forties. There were lines around his eyes and more than a hint of grey in his short blond hair. His stubble was all grey. He was tall with a strong build and Nordic good-looks with pale eyes, a long, straight nose, sharp jawline and a wide, humourless mouth. There was something quite stern about him. He was handsome, no doubt, if Harry were into older guys, which he really wasn't. His last boyfriend, at thirty-six, had been the oldest man Harry had ever been with. Still, Christian looked good for his age.

"You're the captain," Christian said, turning his camera back to the shore. "You know what's best."

Another surprise. Most private charters would bitch and moan the entire way home if Harry told them he'd have to cut the trip short because of bad weather — the same dudes who then turned green and threw up the beer they'd been drinking as soon as the sea turned choppy.

Well, he thought, *whatever happens tomorrow, Christian is proving himself to be a near-perfect client.*

Harry put the boat into a measured turn and headed south.

Christian had drunk nothing but bottled water or tea all day, and he didn't look like the type who'd get sick in a swell, but it was better to be safe. Harry wanted to get him ashore before things turned ugly.

Tom climbed out of the tiny galley, where he'd been clearing away the lunch supplies. "Are we heading in already?"

Harry nodded. "Looks like it's cutting in faster than forecasted. We'll get a better shot tomorrow."

Tom glanced to seaward and nodded before walking out onto the back deck. "Yeah, you can feel the swell is getting up."

"We'll get home before the worst of it," Harry said, with more confidence than he felt.

At thirty-three, Tom was four years older than him, but for as long as he could remember, Harry had always been the more mature and level-headed of them.

Tom sauntered over to Christian, who put down his camera.

"So, what's all this in aid of?" Tom asked. "Most people who hire the boat want to catch fish, not take pictures.

"Tom," Harry warned, "that's none of our business." And to Christian, "Sorry."

The older man gave a slight grin. "It's fine. I don't mind. I'm doing research."

"Research. What? You mean, for like, TV or something?"

Harry smiled. His cousin had never been the sharpest of men. Christian apparently took it in good nature.

"It's for a book."

"Oh, I don't read much." He shuffled his feet. "So, what's your book about? Fishing?"

Christian shook his head. "No, not fishing. I'm not sure what it's about. That's why I'm here. I'm thinking about setting a story somewhere along this coast. Maybe in a town like Nyemouth. I don't know yet."

Tom looked at Harry, a goofy grin plastered across his face. "You hear that? He wants to write a book about Nyemouth."

"*Set* in Nyemouth," Christian corrected. "Maybe. Like I said, I'm not sure. I'm looking for inspiration. Just trying to get ideas for now."

"You've come to the right place," Harry told him.

"Yeah," Tom agreed. "We've got it all going on here."

Christian smiled. It crinkled his eyes even further and revealed good white teeth. It was a very attractive smile.

For an older man, Harry reminded himself.

"Is that so?"

"Hell, yeah." Tom bounced with excitement. "If I tell you about it, will you put me in your book? Like, as a character."

Christian chuckled, humouring him in a good-natured way. "We'll see. I can give you an acknowledgement…if your information is good."

Harry listened as his cousin ran his mouth, content to steer the boat without contributing.

"For a little town, we've had so much shit going on that most people wouldn't believe it—murders, attempted murders, drowning. Whatever you can think of, it's happened here. Just this summer, the UK Border Forces intercepted a fishing boat coming into the harbour. They found sixty-nine migrants hidden in the hold. The boat had come over from Belgium. They must have figured it was easier to smuggle people onto the quieter north coast than down south, where everyone is watching for them. That caused quite a stir. And just last year, a local businessman tried to murder his husband on a yacht just outside the harbour. And before that, someone tried to kill Arnie Walker, you know, the actor, on the north shore beach. You should put all that in your book."

Christian nodded, zipping his jacket. The wind had increased. "I know Arnie Walker—and his husband, Dominic. They are the main reason I'm here. When I told Dominic I was thinking about setting a book in Northumberland, he suggested I check out this area."

"Oh, that's right. Dominic's a writer, too. I always forget that. He doesn't use his own name." Harry looked at Christian in a new light. Dominic Melton was one of the nicest men he knew, brave and dependable. If Christian was a friend of his, there had to be something good about him.

"That's how we met," Christian said, turning his cool grey eyes towards him. "At a literary festival about three years ago. We've kept in touch, though this is my first time in Nyemouth."

"So, are you staying with Dominic and Arnie?" Tom asked.

"No. I've got a room at Quay House. Nothing against the guys and their lovely home, but I like my privacy at the end of the day. I can never relax when I'm in someone else's place."

Harry understood that well enough. He'd lived on his own since leaving his parents and couldn't imagine the compromise involved in sharing with someone else.

"What kind of books do you write? The same kind of stuff as Dominic?"

He shook his head. "Dominic's novels are more action-oriented. I write crime stories, murder mysteries — that kind of thing."

"What did I say?" Tom blurted excitedly. "You've definitely come to the right place."

"Not from what I've seen so far. Nyemouth seems a quiet, laid-back kind of town."

"It's really not," Tom said.

"When did you arrive?" Harry asked.

"I got here on Saturday afternoon."

"Give it time," Tom told him. "You haven't seen anything yet."

"Give it a rest, Tom," Harry admonished. "It's not that bad, honestly. There have been a few incidents over the years, but no more than any other place. I bet if you scratch the surface of any small town, you'll find plenty of similar stories."

"I know," Christian said with a knowing smile.

The winds increased, and the boat swayed farther in the swell. The weather was changing much faster than he'd expected. A few heavy splats of rain landed on the deck.

"Things are about to get choppy," Harry told Christian. "Come into the wheelhouse. You'll be sheltered from the worst of it." He told Tom to brew another round of tea.

As Christian stepped inside, the rain started in full and was soon bouncing several inches off the wooden decking.

"Is it always so unpredictable?" he asked.

"Yep. The only thing you should expect at sea is the unexpected. I'm going to have to pick the speed up a bit if we're going to outrun the worst of it. That means it's going to get bumpy. Hold on to something and watch your footing."

Harry pushed the throttle. The front and back pitch of the boat increased as it ploughed through the strengthening waves. He estimated they were forty minutes out from Nyemouth Harbour. *The North Star* was an old vessel, but she was sturdy. She could handle a lot worse than this and had done so many times, but when people chartered the boat, he had a responsibility to them. Though some captains might take a different attitude, Harry wasn't in business to make his clients sick or frighten them in high seas. He would get Christian back to shore before the worst struck, even if the ride was a little uncomfortable.

He glanced over his shoulder at the older man. He looked to be bearing up okay. Christian stared at the worsening conditions with seeming curiosity. There was no sign of anxiety.

Tom returned with three mugs of tea, distributing them without spilling a drop.

"There's a bottle of whisky below," Harry said to Christian, "if you fancy a tot to keep the cold out."

"This is fine. Thank you."

Satisfied that the client wasn't about to freak out on him or fall over and break something, Harry gave all his concentration to the boat and route ahead. The wind blew hard against the port side, but they were far enough from shore that he didn't have to worry about it blowing them off course or onto the rocks. When he reached the entrance to the harbour, the force of it would be behind them and shouldn't cause much trouble.

"What do you do when you're not running private charters?" Christian asked.

"Sightseeing mostly," Harry answered. "During the summer, I run a variety of different excursions along the coast. Bird watching, half-day fishing trips, twilight cocktail parties...anything to get the tourists on board. I have a few private charters to keep me going over the coming weeks, but once we get into deep winter, I'll spend my time maintaining the boat and getting ready for next spring."

"Have you been out here long? Working on the boat, I mean?"

"My whole life. It used to belong to my dad. He was a fisherman, and I grew up on this thing, going out most weekends and every day during the holidays. He retired four years ago, due to his health. Fishing full-time isn't for me, so I repurposed the boat for the tourist market. I've been running these trips ever since." He glanced over his shoulder at Christian. "You're not going to use *me* in one of your books, are you?"

Tom laughed. "You wish he would."

Christian gave another of his cracking smiles. It completely changed the appearance of his otherwise down-turned features. "I don't know what I'm going to write about yet—or whom. I'll let you know. So, with all these exciting things happening around Nyemouth, have you ever been caught up in any of them yourself?"

He turned back to the view ahead. "I crewed on the lifeboat when I was younger, but not as much as I wanted to. I was at sea so much myself that I was rarely available when they had a call out. It was also a struggle to keep up with the training demands. We had some hairy rescues, all the same. We once evacuated the entire crew of a trawler just minutes before she sank."

He pointed ahead. "They were so close to the shore when they went down, about a mile from the harbour. They had taken on so much water there was nothing we could do. We might not have saved the boat, but we got the crew home safely to their families that night."

"That's what really matters."

"Right."

"I think maybe there is a book here. Everyone I've spoken to seems to have an interesting story to tell."

Harry shrugged. "Maybe. I don't think about it that way. It's all part of life."

The boat took a sudden lurch to starboard as a heavy wave struck them, side on. Christian crashed against the wall of the wheelhouse and hissed as he spilt his tea.

"Sorry," Harry said, getting the boat under control. "Are you both okay?"

"I'm fine," Christian said, "though it's maybe more excitement than I bargained for."

"It won't be long now. If you look ahead and to the right, you can make out the harbour walls and the lighthouse. We're almost home."

They carried on in silence for the rest of the journey. Harry hoped the freak wave hadn't startled Christian enough for him to cancel tomorrow's trip. This shitty front was forecast to blow over during the night, and the outlook for the morning was good. He'd take him to The Fisherman's Arms when they got back to make up for the shortened trip and persuade him to stick to his plan.

There was now less than half a mile to the harbour entrance. *Almost there.*

"Wait!" Christian shouted, stepping forward. He came up beside Harry and stared through the rain-lashed window.

"What is it?" Harry tried to follow his eyeline.

"I'm not sure. I thought I saw something."

Harry eased back on the throttle. "What kind of something?"

Christian chewed his thumbnail. "I'm not sure. I thought for a second it was…a person in the water. I don't know. Maybe…"

Harry's pulse quickened in an instant. "Where?"

Christian pointed. The surface of the sea was a turbulent mass of dark-grey waves and deep swells. Harry reduced their speed even further, causing the boat to pitch and roll dramatically. Tom went onto the deck and scrabbled around the wheelhouse to the bow for a better view.

"When the sea is like this, it can play tricks on the eyes," Harry said. "Are you sure?"

Christian narrowed his eyes, straining to see. "No. I'm not sure. It's just—*there*." He lurched forward, pointing.

Harry saw it at the exact same time on the upward sweep of a wave, the unmistakable shape of someone's head and shoulders. The waves crashed, and they vanished from sight in the next second. He altered course.

If there was someone in the water this far out, they were already in big trouble.

Chapter Two

The muscles in Christian's belly tightened. The second he realised there was a person in the water, adrenaline surged through him then everything happened very fast. Displaying remarkable control, Harry grabbed the radio and put in an immediate call to the coastguard, stating their position.

"There is at least one casualty in the water," Harry told them.

How can he stay so calm? Christian wondered. He could only guess it was through years of experience at sea.

Harry's eyes stayed fixed on the view ahead. "Shout out as soon as you see anything," he instructed.

Christian nodded. They had more or less reached the location where he'd last seen the casualty. Harry brought the boat down slow. Without propulsion, the vessel was tossed upon the waves, pitching front to back and rolling side to side. From the bow, Tom scanned the water in front of them. Christian stepped onto the open deck at the rear. He had never felt so helpless.

"Where are you going?" Harry asked.

"The more eyes out there, the better."

"Be careful. I don't want two people in the water." Harry's voice was stern. "Hold on to the railing."

As soon as he spoke, the boat took a dramatic turn to the side. Christian grabbed the rail with both hands, gripping tight. Rain lashed against his head and shoulders and the wind tore around him. While it had been obvious from the cabin that conditions were worsening, he'd had no idea they'd gotten this bad until Harry had reduced their speed. Whoever was in the sea right now, their chances were diminishing by the second.

As a reporter, Christian had spent his entire career chasing stories that had already played out, arriving on the scene when the danger had passed and reporting on the facts. He had never been this deep in an incident as it unfolded. It was an unnerving experience, and despite having reported on terrorist attacks, riots and major road collisions, he felt ill-equipped to handle it.

Unlike Harry.

He glanced at the younger man as he craned his neck from side to side, checking in every direction, and marvelled again at his composure. It was exactly what was needed. Despite his age, Harry had more than proved his ability to captain a boat.

"This way," Tom shouted from the front, gesturing with his right hand. "Two o'clock. About twenty-five yards."

Harry increased the throttle gently. Tom hurried down the length of the boat and jumped onto the deck beside Christian.

"He's coming up on this side," Tom said. "I'm going to need your help to pull him onboard."

Christian nodded, gripping the rail as he leaned over the edge, trying to spot the casualty.

And there he was. A tiny head and one arm above the surface. The boat slowed as it approached. The man appeared unconscious. His eyes were closed, and his skin was a ghastly grey colour. His lips were almost blue. He wouldn't last long if they didn't get him out of there.

"Keep hold of the rail with one hand," Tom instructed, "and help me with the other."

Christian realised why a second later. As the boat came to a near stop, it pitched so far to the right he would have gone straight over if he hadn't been gripping tight. His feet skidded beneath him, but he managed to keep his balance, steadying himself just as they came alongside the casualty in the water.

There was no response from the man as Tom leaned over and grabbed his jacket by the collar, pulling him against the side of the boat.

"All right," Tom said, "*now*."

Christian leaned down and grabbed the man's jacket from the other side. A wave washed over them, and he realised just how cold the sea was. No one would survive in that temperature for long, even without the terrifying swells and lethal currents. They pulled. The man was a dead weight. With another heave, Christian hooked his elbow into the man's armpit.

"Good," Tom shouted as wind, rain and seawater battered their faces. "On the count of three, we'll try to pull him in. One. Two. Three."

They heaved. The muscles in Christian's shoulders and back screamed with the effort. They barely managed to raise him a few inches from the side before he slipped back again. The force of another wave threatened to carry him away, but Christian held on, keeping the man close to the boat.

"Again," Tom cried.

On the count of three, they gave another heave.

This time, the sea worked in their favour. As they pulled, a large wave surged along the side of the boat, lifting the man upwards. Instinctively, Christian snatched the advantage, pulling the man higher until he grabbed his belt. Tom made similar gains, and with another mammoth heave, they hauled him over the railing and onto the deck.

Christian feared he was already dead, but his knowledge of first aid and his instinct to save a life kicked in.

"Get blankets, towels…anything we can use to warm him up," he shouted at Tom.

As the younger man hurried inside, Christian checked his vital signs. He grabbed the man's wrist, searching for a pulse while putting his cheek close to his mouth, hoping to discern a tell-tale breath. There was nothing. He did not give up. Hypothermia would cause the body to shut down, but it didn't mean the man was finished yet. He appeared young, in his early-to-mid-twenties and strong.

He wore a black padded jacket. It was completely waterlogged. It would have to come off if they were to stand any chance of warming him up. Christian reached for the zipper. His own fingers were numb with cold, and it took three attempts to get a grip and pull it down.

Harry came out of the cabin with a bundle of blankets and a first-aid kid. Christian looked up and saw Tom had taken the wheel. It made sense. With a background in the lifeboat service, Harry would be better equipped than any of them to help this man.

"Any vital signs?" he asked, kneeling beside Christian.

"None that I can make out." He still struggled with the zipper and had only got it down as far as the chest.

Harry pressed his fingers in the crease of the man's neck while Christian used two hands to pull the zipper of his jacket down.

"There's something. I think. It's faint, but I can feel a pulse." Harry spread out the blankets. "Let's get the jacket off and try to warm him up."

Christian unfastened the zipper completely and peeled back the waterlogged sides of his jacket. The man wore a grey T-shirt. At first glance, he thought the red stain across the abdomen was part of a design but only for a second. He eased the bottom of the T-shirt away from his skin.

"He's bleeding," he cried, lifting the garment to expose the full extent of the wound. There was a two-inch laceration above and to the right of the man's navel. The wound was clean, and the cold water must have stopped the worst of the bleeding, but as he watched, bright red blood rose to the surface and spilt over.

Christian slapped his hands on top of the injury and pressed down hard.

Harry tore into the first-aid pack and handed him a fresh dressing. "Use this. Apply as much pressure as you can." He turned and shouted to Tom. "Radio an update. Tell them the casualty is alive but in serious condition. Abdominal injury. He's lost an unknown amount of blood and is displaying advanced hypothermia."

Christian's hands were already red when he lifted them to apply the thick pad and pressed down again. "I think… I think he's been stabbed. It's a knife wound."

Harry's expression was grim. "It sure looks that way. Just keep doing what you're doing." Displaying incredible strength, Harry eased the man's shoulders from the deck and whipped the sodden coat out from under him. One-handed, he slung a blanket around him and eased him down. He laid a towel across his chest and, after checking his limbs for further wounds, covered his lower body with another blanket. Returning to the head, he opened one of the man's eyes with his thumb.

"Niko," he shouted. "Niko, can you hear me?" There was no response. Harry pressed his cheek close to the man's mouth, checking for breath like Christian had done. "Niko, you're safe now. We're heading in. We'll have you ashore soon."

"You know who he is?" Christian asked, impressed by Harry's calm, commanding behaviour. Christian could barely keep his own nerves under control, but the attitude of the young captain kept him focused.

"Yes…Niko," he said, cradling the man's head. "He works at one of the bars in town."

Christian looked down at his hands. There was blood everywhere. "He's losing a lot," he said, keeping his voice low in case, by some miracle, Niko could hear him.

"The lifeboat is coming," Tom hollered from the wheelhouse. "Just leaving the harbour walls."

"It won't be long now," Harry said, soothing the unconscious man's brow. "Help is on the way."

Christian glanced at Niko's face. His pallor was ghastly. He pressed harder on his abdomen in a desperate effort to stop him from losing any more blood. He looked so young. It was difficult to gauge with his grey skin and lips, but he could only be in his early twenties. *Just a boy.* Who the hell could have done this? Christian was no expert, but he was sure the boy had been stabbed. That was the only explanation for the neatness of the wound. It was impossible for him to have sustained such a clean injury as a result of falling into the sea. When the police examined the jacket, he had no doubt they would find a similar straight cut. The padding might even have prevented the blade from inflicting greater damage, not that it looked like it had done him much good. They might have rescued him from the water, but the boy was in deep trouble.

Christian was aware of the boat slowing down again and the sound of an approaching engine.

Harry eased Niko's head to the deck and clambered to his feet. "You're doing brilliantly," he told Christian. "Keep it up. I'll be right back."

He hurried to the railing and reached over as the lifeboat came alongside. The two boats ran parallel to each other, matching their speed. One of the crew, dressed in a waterproof uniform and wearing a safety helmet, stood on the side of the lifeboat, preparing to jump. It was a perilous manoeuvre, as the swell caused the two boats to rise and fall dramatically. One second, the lifeboat appeared to be ten feet above them and the next it had disappeared from sight.

At that moment, Christian realised that their efforts were in vain.

Niko's blood had stopped pulsing through his fingers. He knew the boy had gone but did not release his hold, clinging to the hope that he was wrong and the lifeboat crew could do something…anything.

In the fraction of a second that the two boats came in line, the rescuer leapt across, grabbing onto the railing. Harry helped them onboard. Christian heard him filling the new arrival in on the situation. The figure crouched beside Christian. He couldn't make out a single feature beneath the bright yellow waterproofs and helmet.

"Keep the pressure on the wound until I've assessed him." The voice was male. He moved around to Niko's head and opened his eyes, shining a small torch into his pupils. "Niko, my name is Jake. I need to check you over, okay? Try to make a noise if you can hear me."

There was no response. Jake hurriedly dived into the large first-aid case he'd brought and pulled out an Ambu bag resuscitator. He fastened it over Niko's mouth and nose and squeezed air into him.

"Harry," Jake shouted, "start chest compressions. You know what to do, right?"

Harry nodded, dropping to the deck beside the boy. He pulled off the blanket to expose his chest and started the compressions without a pause.

Jake then shouted at Tom. "We don't have time to wait for the helicopter, and we can't lift him off in this condition. Get us to the harbour as quickly as you can." He then began relaying instruction through his headset to the other boat. Christian only made out certain words. *Not breathing. No pulse. Hypothermia. Paramedics.*

The urge to panic returned. He looked at Harry and the determined expression on his face as he pumped up and down on the young man's chest. Niko's life depended on them and what they did next. Christian couldn't lose his shit, not now. There would be time enough for that when they were all ashore. He had a job to do, and though a large part of him knew that it was too late, he clung to hope.

The boat made a terrifying bang each time it came down from another wave. Christian thought it was about to fall apart under the pressure as Tom sped towards land. *How far out are we?* he wondered. Harry had said earlier that they were close to shore, but the journey in seemed to take forever.

Suddenly, the trembling and rattling ceased. Christian looked up as the boat slipped into the protective walls of Nyemouth Harbour. They had made it.

Please, don't let us be too late.

Chapter Three

Christian saw the blue lights of an ambulance flashing on the dock. Tom steered the boat and brought it in directly beneath the waiting paramedics. A grey-haired man in his seventies, wearing a fisherman's cap, threw down a rope and Tom secured it to the front of the vessel. As soon as they tied a second rope to the stern, the paramedics scuttled down the rusty ladder and climbed aboard.

Christian had never known such a feeling of complete helplessness. All he could do was maintain the pressure on Niko's wound as Jake, the young man from the lifeboat, filled them in on the casualty's's condition and progress. He didn't stop pumping air into his lungs with the Ambu bag. Christian wondered what good it could do now. Niko looked pretty lifeless.

One of the paramedics asked Christian to step aside as they took over his care.

It was pouring. The rain mingled with the young man's blood before washing it over the side. Christian held out his hands, palms upwards, and let the rain rinse them clean. He rubbed his eyes, clearing his sight.

"Hey, fella," a voice called from above.

It was the old man who had thrown the ropes down. Christian realised he was talking to him.

The man beckoned him to the ladder. "Come on up. Let's get you dried off and warmed up."

Christian looked down again. Harry, Jake and the two paramedics continued to work on Niko. He couldn't see anything of the wounded man besides his legs. There was nothing he could do except get in their way. He stepped across the slippery deck, gripping the handrail to keep upright, and made it to the ladders.

"That's it," the old man said, taking his hand when he reached the top and helping him up. Sharp eyes looked at Christian from a kind face. "Let them do their jobs. You come with me." He put his hand on Christian's shoulder and led him to the lifeboat station.

The old man's compassion threatened to overwhelm him as they stepped out of the wind and rain. Tears pricked Christian's eyes as his body released the tension he'd been holding.

The man introduced himself. "I'm Jacob. Come on, this way. You've had a shock. You need to get warm."

Despite the awful conditions, a curious crowd had gathered in front of the station. Christian was aware of them watching as Jacob guided him inside. One man in fishing waterproofs seemed nosier than the rest. "What's going on, Jacob?" he shouted above the wind.

The older man either didn't hear the question or pretended not to and passed without comment.

The lifeboat was still in the water and the station seemed cavernous and empty without it. Jacob took him through a door marked 'Private', into a cosy kitchen and sitting area. It seemed so small and mundane after what he had just been through. Jacob opened a cupboard and handed him a couple of towels. Christian took them gratefully and wiped his face and neck before drying his hair.

Jacob filled the kettle and put it on to boil. "We'll get an update in a little while. I expect the police will want to speak to you before you leave."

Christian nodded. "I'm still trying to process what happened. It... Well, it hasn't sunk in yet."

"That's no surprise. You've had an enormous shock. Sit down. Don't force it." He put a tea bag into a mug and spooned in two sugars. "You were on a charter with Harry?"

Christian nodded, dropping gratefully onto the sofa in the corner. "It was a sightseeing trip more than anything. We were heading back when I spotted something in the water. I didn't even know it was a person at first."

"It's lucky that you did. It's hard to spot someone in calm conditions, never mind a horror like this afternoon."

"I think...he's been stabbed." The words sounded incredulous, even as he said them. Christian's mind flashed back to the wound he'd found beneath Niko's clothes. "It couldn't have... Well, I don't think he could have sustained that injury any other way."

Jacob sighed. "I heard it over the radio. It seems hard to believe, but I've been working around this station my whole life, and there's very little that surprises me anymore. When the crew goes out in that boat, they're trained to expect the unexpected."

"Shit. He looked so young, too. Just a kid, really."

"Don't dwell on that. You saw him. If it wasn't for you, he would still be out there with no one to take care of him. That's what you have to remember." The kettle came to the boil. Jacob made the tea and added a good splash of milk. He brought the mug to Christian with a plate of biscuits. "Eat these. The sugar is good for shock. You'll need it."

Christian thanked him. The biscuits were dry and difficult to swallow, but with a slurp of hot tea, he got them down. As he raised the mug to his mouth, he realised how badly his hand was shaking.

He jerked his head as the door of the crew room opened. It was Harry. The young man looked like he'd aged ten years since Christian had last seen him. His wet hair was plastered to his face. Water ran down his brow and dripped from the end of his nose and chin. His clothes clung to his body. Exhaustion was written clear across his face. Jacob brought him another towel and told him to sit.

"How is he?" Christian asked. "Niko?"

Harry opened his mouth to speak and faltered. He swallowed and inhaled before slowly shaking his head.

"Shit," Christian gasped.

"Oh, no." Jacob sagged against the kitchen counter.

The boy was dead. Suddenly, nothing seemed real. A heavy pulse sounded in Christian's head, obscuring everything, and for a moment, he felt detached from it all, floating in another space and time. Harry's voice snapped him back to the present.

"There was nothing the paramedics could do. They think we lost him out there. He was dead by the time we brought him in."

Hot, silent tears rolled down Christian's cheeks. "He was alive when we pulled him onboard."

"Don't blame yourselves," Jacob said, "either of you. You did everything you could. You brought him home. Without you, his family would be left wondering where he was tonight."

Wherever they thought he was, Christian couldn't imagine it was dead on the deck of a tourist boat. *Jesus*. The poor people likely had no idea yet — not until they received the knock on the door that no one ever wanted to receive.

"Are you all right?" he asked Harry.

The nod was almost imperceptible. "When I was on the crew here, the aim was always to bring them back alive. The alternative is never easy."

"No, but you were great. You did everything possible," Christian told him. "From the moment we saw him, you were calm and decisive. I wouldn't have been the same in your position. I think…the damage was already done. He must have lost so much blood in the water. He was barely alive when we found him."

Harry turned to look at him. His eyes were moist and dark with sorrow. For the first time, Christian noticed the shades of hazelnut flecked with amber within them. Instinctively, Christian put his arm around Harry's shoulder and pulled him close. Harry fell against him without resistance, and they stayed like that for several minutes. There was no need to speak. They took comfort from each other as they dealt with their deep, mutual sadness.

The spell was broken when the door opened again. As he came inside, Tom looked even more beaten down and weary than Harry did.

"They police are here," he said. "They want statements from all of us."

"Okay." Harry made a move to stand.

"No," Jacob said. "You're wet, freezing and in shock. You're not going back out there yet. Stay here. Have another cup of tea. I'll tell the police they can speak to you in here." He refilled the kettle and passed another towel to Tom. "Sit by the radiator. Get warmed up."

Jacob left, and Tom did as he was asked. Christian, who had thawed out more than the other two, got up and set about making another round of tea.

"What are they saying now?" Harry asked.

"Not much." Tom's voice was flat, like he was disconnected from it all. "There's a real fucking crowd at the door of the station, though. News travels fast. It's just as well we stay in here out of the way. Stew Wallace is stopping everyone he sees, wanting to know what happened. He's a fucking old gossip. Got nothing better to do than talk about other people. He'll be in the pub later, holding court and making out like he knows it all. God, he gets on my tits at times, that man."

"Ghouls," Harry muttered. "Are any of Niko's family there?"

"No. They probably don't even know yet."

"I hope the police get to them before any of those nosey bastards do."

Christian handed out the fresh mugs of tea and topped up the plate of biscuits for Tom and Harry. "What did the police say?"

"Not a lot. Just that we shouldn't leave until they've spoken to us."

"It looks like you'll be staying in town then," Harry said as Cristian sat next to him again. "For a while at least."

"I'm here for two weeks, anyway. That's the plan. I'm sure they'll have taken a statement by then, though I don't know what I can tell them besides what I saw."

"None of us can," Tom said. "If Niko was stabbed — and it bloody well looked like he was — it happened before he went into the water. I reckon he must have gone in off one of the piers or somewhere along North Beach. It's the only way he could have drifted out that far. They'll have to focus their investigation in the town."

"How well did you know him?" Christian asked. "Niko?"

Harry shrugged. "Casually, I guess. I think his family came to Nyemouth about twelve years ago. He must have been about eight at the time. But he's been working at the club for a couple of years. That's where I know him from mostly, just from serving behind the bar. He's a friendly enough lad." He paused, seeming to realise what he'd said. "*Was* a friendly lad. Shit."

"Yeah, me, too," Tom said, sounding morose. "Spoke to him behind the bar, even had a few pints together when he was on one of his nights off. Everyone liked him. Well, all the decent folk did, anyway."

Unusual comment, Christian thought, but before he could pursue it further, Jacob returned with two uniformed police officers.

"They won't keep you long," Jacob explained. "They only need the bare facts tonight."

"We'll need a more detailed statement in the next day or two," the female police officer said, "when we know more, but for tonight, just tell us what you experienced on the boat."

Harry got to his feet. "It's my vessel. I'm the captain. If you start with me, I can give all the details of our position and timing."

"That sounds like a good idea," she said.

Jacob gave them the use of the upstairs office to conduct the interviews.

Christian warmed up while he waited for his turn. His clothes had more of less dried, and he had lost track of the time he'd spent in the kitchen. The small room with three people inside grew stuffy and unbearably hot. He needed fresh air. He motioned to Tom that he was stepping out for a few minutes.

Tom was on the phone to his wife and gave him a thumbs-up without breaking their conversation.

The lifeboat, on its trailer, was back in the station. The crew was busy on board, cleaning down and preparing the boat for its next emergency. Christian edged his way around to the front doors. It was full dark now, and a furious wind howled through the marina, but it had not deterred the hardy crowd of observers outside. News of a potential murder had stirred them into action. He watched as they huddled together against the storm, gossiping and speculating on what had gone down. As a journalist, he'd seen it a hundred times before. Wherever there was trouble, he would find a crowd of spectators. Nyemouth was no different from anywhere else.

He spotted the man in waterproofs from earlier. He had drawn a small crowd of his own. Was this the guy Tom had spoken about earlier? The town gossip? *It looks that way.* He was in his mid-fifties with a weathered face and the bulbous snout of a heavy drinker.

Christian shuffled away before the man spotted him.

It was almost eight o'clock. He didn't know how long he'd been here. It must have been hours, though it felt like no time at all since he'd spotted the dark shape in the sea ahead of them. *Time enough for a man to die, for the lives of his family to be changed forever.*

His thoughts were interrupted by a gentle hand on his arm. He turned and met the welcome gaze of his friend, Dominic Melton. Without words, Dominic opened his arms and Christian stepped in for a hug. He wanted to stay there. In a strange town, on the most surreal and stressful day of his life, Dominic offered a glimmer of comfort and protection.

"How are you doing?" Dominic asked, squeezing him tight.

Christian sighed and closed his eyes for a moment. "Truthfully, I don't know. Functioning, barely."

"It must have been a hell of shock," Dominic said. "For an awful moment, when the call came in from *The North Star*, I thought it was you who had fallen overboard."

Christian stood back from him. "Wait! You were on the lifeboat."

He nodded. "At the helm."

With their waterproof uniforms and headgear, it was difficult to tell one member of the crew from another. It hadn't occurred to him that his friend might be one of them. Then again, there had been no time to think about much of anything.

"I'm sorry," Christian said, remembering what Harry had told him about going to sea to save lives, "that it didn't work out."

"You have nothing to apologise for, so stop thinking like that. Okay? It's bullshit."

He nodded. "I know. I just…keep seeing that boy on the deck."

As another surge of emotion threatened to take him, Christian fought against it. He had to keep it together. He wasn't the one who had lost a son or a brother today. For the sake of Niko's family, he would keep his head straight and tell the police everything he remembered.

"Do you want to stay with us tonight? Arnie and AJ are home. We can order a takeaway. There's plenty of room. The spare bed is always made up."

Christian smiled appreciatively. "You're very kind. Thanks for the offer, but I don't know what time I'll be finished here. The police still need a statement from me."

"You can come up any time…however late."

"I'm grateful, but I don't feel like I'll be much company. When I'm done here, I intend to down so much whisky that I'll sleep soundly through to morning. I'll be fine at the hotel."

"Okay, I won't push it. But if you change your mind, call me, whatever time it is. I'll be there. And I have a good supply of quality whisky, too."

"Noted. You're a good friend."

"You're still coming to dinner tomorrow night, though. No excuses. We're all looking forward to it."

"I am, too. Nothing will keep me away from that."

Before he could get teary-eyed again, Harry came out of the crew room. The poor guy looked even more tired than when he'd seen him last. Christian couldn't remember ever seeing a face so sad. "They're ready for you," he said.

"Okay." Christian patted Dominic's arm. "See you tomorrow."

"Don't be late," Dominic said, returning the pat before walking away.

"How was it?" Christian asked Harry.

The younger man's shoulders sagged. "I've given them the facts. All they want is your side of the story."

"You look done in. Are you going now?"

His mouth widened into a weary smile. "I'll wait until you're finished."

"You don't have to. I'll be fine. You should get some rest. I'll go back to my hotel after this."

Harry fixed him with his soulful eyes. "I want to see this through. You were my responsibility today. I owe you. I'll wait until you're done."

Christian was about to argue otherwise but stopped himself. Although Dominic had invited him to spend the night with his family, Harry and Tom were the only people who really understood what they had been through. Maybe they needed to be together to make sense of it.

"Okay. Thanks. I'll buy you a drink when we're finished. I think we'll need it."

Chapter Four

Harry waited outside. The crowd of onlookers had just about dispersed, though Stew Wallace wanted to know all the gory details. Stew was a fisherman from the same generation as Harry's dad, and Harry had known him all his life. Not much went on in the community that Stew didn't know about, and if he didn't, he made it a priority to find out. Harry had never been keen on the man. Growing up, he'd found him an overbearing bore. Little had changed. His dad had always said Stew was like an old hen, pecking around other people's business. The fact he'd also displayed misogynistic and racists traits had done little to endear him.

"So, you spotted him about a mile off North Point, eh?" Stew edged into Harry's personal space.

Harry couldn't decide what smelled worse, the coffee and onion on Stew's breath or the stale, damp stink coming off his ancient flat cap. He turned his head away, inhaling the vigorous sea air.

"Not as far as that," he answered, "but there about."

Stew nodded gleefully, scrunching up his weathered face. He knew this already. He'd spent the last hour flitting from one member of the lifeboat crew to another, gathering details. By the morning, these titbits would be embellished, exaggerated and passed on as facts.

"So, what was he like when you pulled him aboard? Guts hanging out, were they? I heard he was filleted like a fish."

"For fuck's sake, Stew, give it rest. That lad has a family who'll be devastated right now. They can do without this bullshit. Show a bit of respect."

Stew smarted. He widened his eyes in a comical fashion. "Keep your knickers on. He was stabbed, wasn't he? He's dead now, isn't he? Where's the bullshit in that? Folks want to know what happened. It's only natural."

"Then stick to the facts. Stop making stuff up. It's your sick imagination talking. It's not the truth."

Stew sniffed, then hawked and spat a huge gob of phlegm onto the ground. He bristled his shoulders indignantly. "Still, it doesn't surprise me — being him, I mean. It was only a matter of time before one of these Pols got it. A lot of folk are sick of them. There's just too many of them about these days. I'm surprised someone hasn't done something about them before now."

"Oh, just shut up, will you? I don't want to hear crap like that." Harry had been exposed to Stew's ignorant racism for as long as he could remember. Even when Harry had been a kid, Stew had had no hesitation venting his bigotry in front of him. He didn't want to listen to one more word and turned back into the lifeboat station.

His dad, Jack, was talking to one of the engineers. He broke off as Harry approached.

"How are you doing now, son?" his dad asked, putting a hand on his shoulder. "You looked wiped out."

"I'm all right. Just a bit dazed, that's all."

"The police are still busy on your boat. I don't think we'll be allowed on for a few hours yet."

"I couldn't face it, anyway. Not tonight."

"That's no surprise," Jack said. "Do you want to come home with me tonight? It's probably not a good idea for you to be alone. We can come back down tomorrow, and I'll help you clean the boat down."

Harry smiled. For years, it had irked him that his parents still treated him like a child at times, but after a day like this, their concern was welcome. "Thanks, but I'm going to take Christian for a drink when he's done with the police. I reckon he'll be in a greater state of shock than I am. The poor bloke hired me for a day of sightseeing and ended up helping to bring a body home."

"Where is he staying? In town?"

"At Quay House. I think that's what he said. On his own, too. I'll take him for a few pints and see how he's doing. I don't like the idea of anyone going straight back to an empty hotel room. Not after today."

Jack shook Harry's shoulder fondly. "You're a good lad. I'm proud of you. You did great stuff today. Don't beat yourself up over this. You did everything you could. And if you change your mind, call on us after the pub. However late it is, we'll be glad to see you."

Harry choked back his emotions and hugged his dad. He knew how lucky he was to be part of such a loving family. And all of them were safe tonight. Niko Jasinski's family were not so fortunate.

Christian came out of the crew room just before nine, all slouched shoulders and down-turned mouth. The poor man looked exhausted. Harry realised he was probably just as bad, if not worse. Christian looked up and seemed to brighten at the sight of a friendly face.

"Are you okay?" Harry asked, walking towards him.

He wiped his hand across his face, rubbing his eyes. "Yeah. I don't think I told them anything they hadn't already heard from you."

"You'd be surprised. In an emergency, people notice different things. One person can spot something another didn't. I'm sure you were a great help."

He let out a weary exhalation. "I hope so. God, I need a drink. Are you still up for it?"

"Absolutely," Harry answered.

Harry took him to The Fisherman's Arms, a short walk along the marina from the lifeboat station. The worst of the storm seemed to be right over the town, and the wind and rain drove against them as they hurried to the entrance. Monday night and out of season, the place was less than a quarter full. *Good.* Harry didn't want to deal with any more stupid questions from curious locals.

He was pleased to see a fire burning in the hearth. Even better, the two armchairs beside it were empty, and he made straight for them.

"What are you drinking?" Christian asked.

"No, I'm getting them," Harry said. "I owe you for all you've done today."

Christian waved his hand and gestured for him to sit. "You can buy the next round. What will it be?"

"A pint of lager. Thanks."

With a nod and a tired smile, Christian headed to the bar. Harry kept an eye on him. He appeared to be holding up all right. As he gestured for the bartender's attention, he was more like the man he had met that morning.

Jesus. Was that only this morning?

It felt like days ago.

Harry took off his jacket and turned his chair towards the fire, pushing his feet forward to take full advantage of its heat. He wriggled his icy toes, wondering whether he would ever feel warm again. He took out his phone and found he had sixteen missed calls and thirty-seven text messages. *Shit.* It didn't take a genius to work out what they all wanted. He'd already spoken with his parents, so anyone else could wait until tomorrow. He threw the phone face down onto the table.

Christian returned with two pint glasses — lager for Harry and what looked like a pint of ale for himself. With a tight smile, he set them down before returning to the bar and coming back with two tumblers of whisky. "I don't know about you, but I need something else to take the edge off, not to mention the chill."

Harry nodded, choosing the whisky first. "Come on. Move closer to the fire. It helps."

Christian adjusted his chair until it faced Harry from the other side of the hearth and flopped onto the seat. He picked up his tumbler with a sigh and leaned forward with his glass raised.

"To Niko."

"To Niko," Harry replied, and they clinked glasses.

The whisky was smooth, expensive and deliciously warm as it went down.

Christian sank back into his chair, his long legs stretched in front of him and crossed at the ankles. The glow from the fire stressed the strong angles of his face. Harry was taken by how remarkably handsome he was, as if seeing him for the first time.

"Shit day, eh?" Christian's voice was completely deadpan.

Harry let out a short laugh despite himself. "That's a definite understatement. I'd say it's been a complete bastard."

Christian swirled the whisky around his glass before taking a sip. He savoured it before swallowing. Harry did the same. The second mouthful tasted even better than the first.

"I keep seeing the boy's face," Christian said. "How young he looked. It's tragic."

"He'll have been around nineteen, possibly twenty. No older."

"Fuck."

"The blabbermouths are already speculating about what happened," Harry said. "While I waited for you, I heard all kinds of crap theories — serial killers, gangsters, drugs debts, racism. For fuck's sake, this is a small coastal town, not a big, bad city. Still, that last suggestion isn't too far out. There are plenty of bigots around here, though most of them are just keyboard warriors. They've got plenty to say on social media, but I'm not so sure they have the nerve to take it further. Certainly not to do *that*."

"Where is Niko from? Originally."

"The family is from Poland, but they've been here for years. Twelve, at least. Though in small communities like this, anyone not born here will always be considered an outsider. My ex is Polish, too.

He runs a photography and art gallery with his brother on the south bank. They've been here a long time, but they still receive a good amount of abuse. They've had their windows broken more than once."

It occurred to him that some of those missed calls and messages might have come from Antoni. The Polish community was small in Nyemouth, and Antoni would likely be close to the Jasinski family. He would give him a call when he was done here. Right now, he didn't have the energy to go through the events of the day one more time.

"I know a little of what that's like," Christian said. Seeing the curious look Harry gave him, he continued. "My mother is Norwegian. I was raised in Manchester, but she was never allowed to forget she was a foreigner. It was the same for me and my brother and sister. Though our dad is English, we were always reminded that our mother was different and, therefore, so were we. We were treated like we didn't belong. Nothing as bad as you're talking about, though. It was a casual kind of racism, the non-violent sort, but the kind of thing that stays with you for life."

"I'm sorry."

Christian shrugged. "There are ignorant people all around. They walk among us."

"They certainly do. God, I really hope that's not what happened to Niko."

"Probably not. As you say, most racist types are all mouth. It's rare for them to act on their prejudices. To stab another human, like Niko, I would guess there was a bigger reason—jealousy, hatred, rivalry, crime." He laughed gently. "Now I sound like one of your town gossips." He put down his empty whisky glass and picked up his ale.

Harry watched the flickering glow of the fire as it skittered across Christian's face. "I suppose it gives you something for your book."

Christian sipped the beer and licked the foam from his top lip. "Not really. I want to write a novel, not a true crime account."

"I thought you were a journalist."

"That's my day job. I'm very much on holiday and in novelist mode. I'm not looking to capitalise on a tragedy like this."

Harry hid his surprise. He'd expected any writer would want to rake over the gory details, a bit like the ghouls outside the lifeboat station. Then again, Christian was friends with Dominic Melton, also a writer and one of the nicest men he knew. Maybe Harry had judged him too harshly.

When they finished their drinks, he collected the empty glasses. "Same again?"

"Just the whisky this time," Christian answered. "It worked better than the ale."

"I know what you mean."

Harry went to the bar. He didn't know the bartender, so didn't have to face another barrage of questions about Niko's death. "Two of whatever these were," he said, holding up the empty tumblers. "Make them doubles."

He glanced over his shoulder as he waited. Christian gazed into the fire, looking lost in his thoughts. What was it about him? Just this morning Harry had dismissed him as being far too old, but the more time he spent with him and talked to him, Christian's appeal grew stronger. *He can't be that old, anyway*, he reasoned. Ten, maybe eleven years older than he was. It wasn't like fancying someone his dad's age.

Of course, Harry knew what really drove this new attraction to Christian.

Death.

He'd learned from his time in the lifeboat how sex and death went hand in hand. He had taken part in three failed rescues when he had been a member of the crew, and afterwards, he had always wanted sex. It wasn't unusual. He'd even read an article about it — how sex helped people to feel alive after a clash with mortality.

Is that what this is? Do I only fancy him because we didn't save Niko?

As he carried the drinks back to the fire, Harry realised just how much he did want Christian. They had been through a gruelling experience. What better comfort could there be than each other's bodies? He didn't want to go back to his flat on his own and wondered whether Christian felt the same about his lonely hotel room.

Fuck it. One more drink and I'll ask him. The worst he can say is no.

Christian lifted his gaze from the flames when he returned. Their eyes connected and, just for a second, a hint of a smile. "Thanks," he said, accepting the drink.

"Is this your favourite tipple? Whisky?" he asked, sitting down.

"Sometimes. It depends on my mood. But at the end of the night, when I want to unwind, it's the best. I always bring a bottle with me when I'm working away — for a nightcap."

Their eyes locked again, and Harry wondered if there had been a hint of an invitation in the last remark. *Or is it just wishful thinking?*

He had never been good at reading signals.

"What's your hotel like?" he asked in a rush. "I've had a drink at the bar in Quay House, but I've never been upstairs."

Christian's brow furrowed in confusion.

Oh shit. I've judged this all wrong.

Then he smiled. "It's nice. I've got a good-sized room that overlooks the harbour. Actually, it's pretty great." He sipped. "You're welcome to come up, if you'd like to look around. I could also give you that nightcap."

Harry's pulse quickened, and a stiffness developed in his groin. "I'd love to."

This morning he'd been so dismissive about Christian because of his age, and now there was nothing he wanted more than to spend the night in his protective embrace.

Raised voices at the bar caught their attention. Two men in waterproofs had come in, desperate to share their news.

"Two in one day. You would hardly believe it," one of the men said.

"What's this?" the bartender asked.

Harry sat up and twisted in his seat to see who they were. He recognised one of the guys as a regular from the working men's club.

"There's been another murder."

Harry and Christian exchanged a startled look.

"When?" Harry shouted over to the men. "Who is it?"

They turned in his direction.

"Don't know who, but the police are all over the Moor Estate—blue lights, ambulances, the lot. They're saying a young lad has been found dead in his front room. His mother came home late from work and found him. That's what we've heard, anyway."

Harry and Christian stared at each other, open-mouthed.

"This can't be right. Two boys dead in one day," Christian said. "What are the chances?"

"That's not the only thing," the man at the bar said. "He was stabbed, just like that lad on the boat this afternoon. You can't tell me they're not connected."

Harry's jaw hung in amazement.

Two murders in Nyemouth in a single afternoon.

"What the hell is going on in this town?"

As the fire blazed and crackled in the hearth and the storm continued outside, no one offered any answer.

Chapter Five

Christian woke to the sound of seagulls squawking right outside his window. As his heavy head swam into focus, he heard the engines of boats in the marina and traffic on the bridge that joined the north and south banks of the town. Dull grey light diffused the room. He shuffled across the bed and fumbled for his phone on the dresser. It was twenty-five to eight—later than he expected.

He could thank the whisky for that. After saying good night to Harry when they left the pub, he'd come back to the hotel and had another two glasses while scribbling the details of the day in his notebook, his ideas and impressions of what had happened. He had spent some time scrolling through the Facebook page for Nyemouth. Unsurprisingly, the double murders were the only subjects up for discussion. There were no names given to either victim. Their families were at least granted that much respect, but the theories that were dispatched were outrageous. None of the people who posted seemed in possession of the actual facts, but that didn't stop their speculation. Christian had given up around two when he'd finished his drink, brushed his teeth and crawled into bed. He must have gone out in an instant.

He had slept solidly all the way through and, surprisingly, given everything he'd experienced the previous day, there had been no nightmares. He wondered whether Harry had been so lucky.

Harry. What an exceptional young man. He had proved himself in every way yesterday, rising calmly to the challenges they faced. He was quite a hero to Christian.

It had seemed there was a spark between them, too. When they had been in The Fisherman's Arms, the connection had deepened, and it seemed almost certain that Harry wanted to end the difficult day in Christian's bed. And Christian would have welcomed him. He had sworn off casual encounters with men he barely knew, but last night he would have made an exception. They had needed each other, maybe only for a few hours, but it would have been enough.

Harry was far too young for him. Any other time, Christian would have kept well away, but after what they had been through, the difference in their ages seemed irrelevant.

News of the second murder had dampened the flames between them, extinguishing any notions of romance in a second.

Christian groaned and pulled the covers over his shoulders.

When he closed his eyes, Harry was there—those warm brown eyes, full of wisdom beyond their years, the dark-blond hair, sexily dishevelled when he took off his cap and ran his fingers through it. How marvellous it would be to feel his body in bed right now, the naked heat of his skin pressed against Christian's back, his erection pressing to the cleft of Christian's arse. Christian squirmed and tugged at his balls.

Stop it.

He must forget all about it. They'd shared a moment, and it had passed. They didn't take the chance when they'd had it and now it had gone.

He rolled onto his back and stared at the ceiling. Nyemouth. He'd come here looking for ideas for a book and found a double murder.

Last night, he'd told Harry he had no intention of writing about Niko's death. Maybe he'd believed it himself at the time. What kind of writer would he be if he ignored a story he had played such an active role in? He had to use this experience in some way. It was true that he had no interest in writing a journalistic, true-life account, but he might never be so closely embroiled in a story again. This was an opportunity he couldn't waste.

To do what? He had no idea.

He'd come to do research, and that's exactly what he would do. What that research would turn into was a question for another time.

Christian flung back the covers and sprang out of bed, a man with a purpose. The day ahead was clear. He was having dinner with Dominic and his family tonight, but other than that, he had nothing planned. His story was out there. It was up to him to go out and find it.

He strode naked to the window and pulled open the curtains. It was a dull, drizzly morning. The storm had passed, and the water in the harbour was as still as a mirror. Christian opened the sash window and stuck out his head, inhaling the briny air. On the opposite bank, farther downriver, was the lifeboat station. The large front doors were open, but it was too far away to recognise any of the figures outside.

He leaned even farther out, craning his neck. Harry's boat would be docked somewhere here on the north bank. There were a lot of vessels in port, and he couldn't make out *The North Star* among them. Harry had told him he would spend most of the morning on the boat. Once they were given the go-ahead from the police, he and his dad wanted to clean everything down. Christian had been due to go out on another sightseeing trip with him this morning, but they had postponed that to later in the week. Right now, Christian wasn't sure he wanted another day at sea.

A seagull swept past the window. Christian wondered if it was the same one that had woken him up.

He pulled back into the room and lowered the sash, leaving a six-inch gap for fresh air.

It was time for action.

* * * *

At the Seagull Café, Christian ordered a large decaf latte to go and stepped to the end of the counter while he waited for it to be made. The café was almost full, with the majority of customers tucking into full breakfasts or bacon sandwiches. Christian had little an appetite yet, though he realised he'd barely eaten at all yesterday. Maybe later, after the coffee, he would stop somewhere for brunch. Right now, he was eager to get started.

For now, that meant listening.

When he was eavesdropping on the surrounding conversations, there was only one topic of discussion — murder.

"Natalie said it was like something from a horror film. He was laid out in the sitting room like a victim in Scream *or* Halloween. *There was blood everywhere, she said."*

"You can't see anything this morning. There's one of those forensic tents at the front of the house."

"Have you seen the south pier today? Police all over it. I heard that's where the first fella was stabbed and shoved into the water. They must be looking for evidence."

Idle chit-chat. No one seemed to know anything for certain, but they wouldn't let that spoil their fun. It was human nature whenever there had been any kind of violent act in a community. The residents picked over every detail and formed their own opinions. Still, if the police were examining the pier, it would be worth his time to investigate...later. Right now, instinct told him to head back to the lifeboat station.

Christian took his coffee outside and wandered to the edge of the marina. The early drizzle had stopped, though the sky was a bleak shade of grey. After yesterday's storm, it was surprisingly mild, and he unzipped his jacket as he walked along the front.

This was indeed a beautiful place. Dominic hadn't been kidding when he'd suggested it would make a great backdrop for a novel. He wanted to write something in the style of the Nordic noir's he devoured, only with a British twist. This rugged area of the north-east coast seemed perfect for what he had in mind. He wondered whether his fiction could be as intriguing as what was happening for real.

When he reached the open doors of the lifeboat station, he was pleased to spot Dominic and the old man, Jacob, among the people working around the boat. Jacob saw him first and nudged Dominic. They both came towards him.

"Good morning," Jacob said. "How are you doing?"

"Not bad. Better than expected. I slept well, too."

"Glad to hear it," Dominic said.

"You do look brightener than when I last saw you," Jacob said. Without the fisherman's cap he'd previously worn, Christian saw he had a thick head of luxurious grey and white hair and the sharpest blue eyes. He must be somewhere in his mid-seventies, not that it was obvious in the sprightly way he moved. "Tea? Coffee?"

Christian raised his takeaway cup. "I'm fine, thanks."

"Well, I'm ready for one, and I bet you are too, Dominic. Go and have yourselves a break, and I'll bring them out." He headed to the crew room.

"He's quite a character," Christian said.

"He's the lifeblood of this place. He's been volunteering at the station for over fifty years."

Dominic led him around the corner to a wooden bench overlooking the harbour. A sailing boat glided towards the mouth of the river as they sat. Christian looked across to the other side, hoping to spot Harry and *The North Star*, but there were still too many vessels tied up. He didn't know enough about boats to tell them apart.

"Are you really all right?" Dominic asked.

"I think so. Maybe still a little shocked, but it's wearing off."

"I take it you've heard about the other murder?"

"Impossible not to. It's all anyone seems to be talking about. I was in that pub over there when we heard about it. It's shocking, isn't it?"

Dominic gave a little snort through his nostrils and stared at the water. "One time, yes, I might have been shocked, but I've lived here for too long to be surprised by much anymore. After what happened to Arnie and AJ when we first met…" He sighed. "Well, there's not much that shocks me these days."

"Is this place really that bad?"

"No worse than anywhere else, I suppose. Every town has its share of tragedy and violence. And I guess volunteering for the lifeboat has exposed me to more of it than I would have otherwise known about. Still, this is a nice town. I wouldn't be here if it wasn't. And if Arnie had wanted to leave after what happened to him, I would have gone with him in a heartbeat. But I'm also glad we're still here."

"I can't wait to see Arnie and AJ tonight," Christian said. "I'm sorry I knocked you back yesterday. I just didn't feel very sociable."

Dominic patted his thigh. "Nor would I have been if I were you. The guys are looking forward to meeting you, though."

Christian sipped his coffee. "So, what have you heard about the second murder? It seems no one is really clear about the facts."

"Speak to Jacob. He knows everything. Don't ask me how, because I don't have a clue, but he's always the one with information. Nine times out of ten, he's right, too. It's a kid from the Moor Estate. Ike, I think his name was. I don't know him, myself. There's a huge supermarket outside of town and he worked there, so the chances are I'll have seen him around. I don't think the police have released any images yet. But he's young, about twenty-seven, I believe."

"Is there any connection between Ike and Niko?"

Dominic shook his head. "I don't have a clue. This is a small town. The chances are high that they knew each other. But if there's more to it, I don't know."

"Two stabbings, though...in one day. That must be out of the ordinary, even in Nyemouth."

"I'd say. A friend of mine was stabbed to death a few years back by the same bastard who came for Arnie, but he is behind bars. I'm not aware of anything that bad since then."

Christian stared at him incredulously. "Bloody hell, Dominic. Is that true? This town sounds like the modern equivalent of the wild west. How many bodies are there piled up?"

Dominic chuckled. "I'm probably making it sound far worse than it is."

"You weren't kidding when you said it would work well for my book."

"Ah, is that where your mind is headed? You're going to write about this?"

"Not as such, not the death of these young men. That's too distasteful. But I think I've found the perfect backdrop for whatever kind of story I decide to tell."

Jacob came around the corner carrying two steaming mugs. Christian and Dominic shuffled along the bench to make room for him.

"I was just telling Christian about the boy who was killed last night. Did you say his name was Ike?" Dominic asked, accepting a mug from Jacob.

"Ike Meeker," the old man said, sitting down. "He's a supervisor up at Asda. He used to wait on tables at The Lobster Pot when he was younger."

"I don't think I know him."

Christian pulled out his phone and brought up Facebook. It did not surprise him to find no matches for an Ike Meeker in Nyemouth. Facebook was more likely an app for his mother's generation. He tried a few other searches before finding a LinkedIn match with a photograph of a cheerful young Black man. "Is this him?" he asked, passing the phone to Jacob.

Jacob peered at the picture. "Yes. Poor kid. That's him."

Dominic looked at the screen. "Oh, right. Yes, I have seen him around. I remember him from the restaurant. He was very friendly."

"Always," Jacob said. "He was a lovely kid. God, what an awful world. Why would anyone want to harm a boy like that?"

As Christian studied the smiling face again, the most obvious connection between the two men came to mind. "Last night, Harry told me that Niko and other people from the Polish community have experienced prejudice here in Nyemouth. It's just a theory, but with Ike being Black and Niko Polish, you don't think these could be hate crimes, do you?"

Dominic and Jacob exchanged glances, giving it some thought before shaking their heads.

"To stab them for that? I wouldn't have thought so," Dominic said. "There are a lot of arseholes around who have plenty to say on racial issues, but they're all mouth. If anyone turned around and answered them back, they'd be just as likely to run away."

"I agree," Jacob said. "Of course, we don't know what anyone is capable of, but the idiots Dominic is talking about are more likely to share racist content online and spout off to their stupid mates than carry out anything. Not to downplay that, but a stabbing is such a violent thing. It requires close contact and determination. I expect the person or people who did this will have a more personal motive than ingrained bigotry."

Christian wasn't so certain. In the last twenty-four hours, Nyemouth had proved to be a beautiful place with a heart of darkness. *What secrets lurk beneath the charming veneer?* he wondered. Dominic and Jacob lived here. Maybe their perception was misleading. They looked at the town through rose-tinted lenses because they loved it so much. Maybe it would take an outsider to expose the grubby undercurrents that ran through it.

Christian smiled to himself.

He was just the man to do it.

Chapter Six

With the aid of his dad and Tom, Harry had thoroughly scrubbed and cleaned the deck of *The North Star* by late morning. Their work had been interrupted several times by curious passers-by and nosy fishermen, but at last they were done. Harry was used to cleaning the boat of fish blood after a bumper day at sea, but the blood of another man was different — an experience he hoped he would never have to repeat. Even Tom had been quiet, going about the task in morose silence, completely at odds with his usual, gregarious self.

Finally, Harry wound up the hose.

"Thanks for your help," he said. "I wasn't looking forward to doing this. I would hate to have done it alone."

His dad dried his hands on the front of his jeans. "We wouldn't have let you, anyway."

"Yeah," said Tom. "What kind of family do you think we are? We would never have left you on your own."

A sudden surge of emotion made Harry realise just how lucky he was to have such a great family. "Well, after all you've done, lunch is on me. What would you like? Anything at all. No limits."

"I wouldn't say no to a sandwich from the Seagull if you're feeling that generous," his dad said.

"I meant a proper sit-down lunch, not just a sandwich."

Both men shook their heads.

"We stink," Tom said. "And I can't be bothered to go home to wash and change. I'm with your dad. A sandwich will do, and a big caramel latte, if you're feeling extra generous."

Harry agreed. "But only if you let me take you out for a proper lunch one day next week." He grabbed a notepad from the cabin and scrawled their orders. Turkey and stuffing on a white roll for Tom, crab salad on wholemeal for his dad, together with their drinks.

The tide was low. He climbed up the slippery ladder to the dock. "Won't be long. Text me if you think of anything else."

The early drizzle had moved away, though low clouds hung over the town without a chink of sunlight, threatening more rain at any time. There were no more storms in the forecast, at least for the rest of the week. The weekend didn't look too promising, but that could change. What mattered was the next few days were clear. Harry wanted to get the boat back out to sea as soon as possible. Yesterday had been an aberration...a blip. He couldn't let it shape his future. The boat was his livelihood, and he had to get back to it.

It was doubtful Christian would want to resume his excursion along the coast, but Harry had a fishing charter booked in for Friday, and he needed to get back to his best. He intended to take the boat out tomorrow — alone if he had to.

Christian. He wondered how he was getting on.

The older man hadn't been far from his thoughts all morning. As he'd busied himself with physical work, his mind had drifted back to the past night.

How close had they come to going to bed together?

Damn near all the way. In the pub, Harry had been hot and horny for him. He'd recognised the urge for sex for what it was, a longing to defy death. He'd experienced it before, but that didn't mean his desire for Christian wasn't real. Harry would have gone with him willingly, and he'd have had no regrets about it today. Even now, he couldn't deny that he still wanted the guy.

If the news of the second murder hadn't killed the mood, they would have gone through with it.

A double dose of death had beaten the need for life-affirming sex.

It didn't have to defeat him now.

He paused at the edge of the dock and pulled his phone from his pocket. He composed the text quickly, before he had a chance to doubt the wisdom of it.

Hi. How are you today? Fancy catching up later this afternoon? Are you free around five?

It sounded good. Caring, but not too needy. He hit Send and shoved the phone back in jeans.

The worst Christian could say was no. Maybe he had woken this morning, grateful to have dodged a bullet. They could still be friends. Harry was genuinely concerned about him after their experience. Sure, Christian was a journalist and would have encountered far worse violence in his career, but he would be used to reporting on things after they had happened, rather than playing an active part. It would only be natural for him to be affected by what he'd been through.

He wondered what kind of man Christian really was. Yesterday might have fast-tracked them to an intimate place, but they barely knew each other. Their conversations on the boat, prior to finding Niko, had been friendly but professionally distant, and they had both been emotional and raw in the pub afterwards. Neither of them had seen a true representation of the other.

Harry was torn between his need to see Christian again, to sleep with him if the attraction continued and leave him well alone. Life was complicated enough right now. Did he really need a love affair, however brief, to confuse things even more? Christian would be here for a few more days. Surely the best thing to do was to keep their relationship on a simple and professional level.

Harry sighed. *Who the hell even knows what's right or wrong anymore?*

As he crossed the bridge towards the Seagull Café, he spotted a familiar face on the south bank, heading in the other direction—Antoni Nowak, his ex-boyfriend of three years. Harry was familiar with every part of Antoni and had no trouble recognising him from behind.

"Hey," he hollered, hurrying to catch up. "Antoni. Hang on."

Antoni turned and saw him. He raised his hand and came back towards him, his long, rangy legs quickly covering the distance.

Shit. He looks knackered.

Antoni's light-brown hair was dishevelled, sticking up in wild curls on top of his head. He was usually immaculate when he stepped outside. His dark-grey eyes were red rimmed and bloodshot. When he stepped up to Harry, his smile was tight and appeared forced.

"Hey, how are you?" Harry put a comforting hand on his arm. "Sorry I missed your calls last night. It was…well…you know."

Antoni gave an imperceptible nod. The sadness in his eyes was clear. "It's okay. I understand. I know you'll have had a lot of questions to answer — the police and all that."

"Are you all right? I know you're friends with Niko's family."

"I was just with them. His mother Anna, she is devastated. They all are. This…whole thing makes no sense to anyone."

"I know. I've turned it over so many times in my head, and I can't get it straight, either. I'm not even sure I really slept last night. Whenever I shut my eyes… I didn't know Niko well, not like you did, but he seemed like a nice kid."

"He was a good boy — not the kind to bring trouble to his parent's door, you know what I'm saying. Everyone loved him." Antoni let out a long gasp. "I don't know what I can do or say to help them."

"I'm sure they appreciate everything you've done." The Polish community was small in the area, but Harry had seen during his time with Antoni just how supportive and loyal they were to each other. "I'm heading to the Seagull to pick up lunch for my dad and Tom. Have you got time for a coffee? You look like you could do with one. It will do you good to sit down, if only for a few minutes."

Antoni opened his mouth and seemed to be on the verge of making an excuse before he sighed again. "Yes. Five minutes of peace and quiet sounds good."

"Good. Come on."

The café was near full when they arrived. The lunchtime service was well under way. Harry spotted an empty table against the right-side wall and told Antoni to grab it while he went to the counter. He placed the order for sandwiches and drinks to go, together with three slices of delicious looking chocolate cake, and asked for two coffees to drink inside while he waited.

Lizzie, the co-owner, was working the register. "Have a seat. I'll bring them over in a few minutes."

Antoni toyed absently with a sachet of sugar when he returned. His mind was clearly elsewhere. He looked a lot older than his mid-thirties. Harry realised how much weight he had lost since they'd split up last December. He'd always had a slim build, but now he was positively skinny. His cheekbones were razor sharp, and the weight loss had deepened the lines around his eyes.

"Did you get much sleep last night?" Harry asked, pulling out a chair to sit opposite him.

He shook his head. "I eventually drifted off sometime after three, but I was awake before six. I just couldn't seem to shut down the noise and images in my mind."

"Maybe you should go home from here. A couple of hours on the couch will do you good."

"We'll see. I do feel tired now. But I'd rather power through and get a good night's sleep tonight."

"Take care of yourself." Harry's love for Antoni was entirely fraternal. Though they had been together for three years, there had been very little passion, and they had been more like brothers than lovers for the last two years of the relationship. Something had always prevented them from progressing to the next level, and Harry had resisted all of Antoni's requests for them to get a place together. "Let me order you something to eat, too."

"No. I have no appetite at all. I'll eat later." Antoni looked at him across the table. "Don't make a fuss. Please."

"All right, I won't," he said, maintaining an even tone. "How is Roger? Does he know the Jasinski family, too?"

Antoni nodded. "He spent time with them last night. We agreed he would open the gallery today so I could visit them this morning. I should take off after this. He'll need a break."

Lizzie appeared with their coffees...two cappuccinos. "Your food will be around ten minutes. I hope that's okay. We're short in the kitchen, and we've been mad busy so far today."

Harry smiled. "No rush." Then when she left, "Do the police have any idea of what happened yet?"

"Not a clue. They've been trying to build a picture of what Niko did yesterday — where he went and who he saw, before you found him." He paused. "His parents, I think they'd like to speak to you. Not today, they're still too much in shock, but maybe in another day or so, just to hear first-hand what happened."

"Of course." Harry understood where they were coming from and why they would want to know, but there was no way he could tell them exactly what had gone down on the boat, their desperate attempts to save Niko's life and stop him from bleeding out. Families always wanted to know what happened to their loved ones in the last moments of their life. Harry's experiences in the lifeboat had taught him that the raw, uncensored truth rarely brought much comfort to the bereaved. Quite the opposite. He would choose his words carefully. "I'll speak to them when they're ready."

"They will appreciate it." Antoni emptied a sachet of brown sugar into his coffee and stirred. "And now there has been a second death, and the police are stretched even thinner. I hope they don't give up on trying to find out what happened to Niko."

"They won't. You know the local police force is small, but they'll draft in officers from out of the area to help in cases like this. It's horrific, though. Two knife crimes in one day."

"I don't know much about the second attack. Have you heard anything?"

"Only gossip, nothing substantial. You know what people are like here. What they don't know, they make up. From what I heard around the dock this morning, they've been quick to make connections between the victims, whether there is one or not."

"Typical. Who was he? The second victim?"

"Ike Meeker. He works at Asda."

Antoni froze, the coffee cup halfway to his lips. "Ike? What? You mean the boy who used to work at The Lobster Pot?"

"I've no idea about that. As you well know, The Lobster Pot is a bit fancy and beyond my budget. I just know what people are saying. I haven't been able to put a face to the name. I'm not sure I even know him. *Knew* him," he corrected.

Antoni pulled out his phone, tapped the screen, and flicked through several menus. Social media, no doubt. After a few moments, he said, "My God, yes. That's him. Ike. He worked over there for a year, at least."

He turned the screen towards Harry. The photo showed a stocky Black man in his twenties. He had a cheerful smile and one of those short, precise haircuts a lot of young guys wore. "I don't think I know him. Like I said, The Lobster Pot is a bit ritzy for me, and I go to Lidl for most of my groceries." When they had been together, Antoni had often tried to get him to go to the fancy restaurant for special occasions, but Harry was always happier in the pub.

"He's a nice boy. At least, he seemed to be. I only know him from the restaurant, but he was always friendly and attentive. He didn't strike me as the type to get in trouble."

"Maybe he didn't," Harry said. "It could be something personal. You don't think Niko knew him, do you?"

Antoni put the phone down. "I have no idea. There's possibly a six- or seven-year age difference between them, but Niko would know a lot of people from working at the club. He got on well with everyone. They could have known each other." He inhaled and let out a weary sigh. "God, this is just awful. Two families devastated in a single night."

They were both startled by a loud voice from behind them.

"Someone has decided to clean up this shitty town. That's what happened. And it's a fucking good thing, too." There was gloating delight in the words.

Harry looked around and groaned. Dean Bewick and his sister Linda sat side by side at a table in the middle of the room. They had their elbows on the table and their arms folded, self-satisfied smirks plastered across their bovine faces. The table was littered with the debris of their lunches, with more sauce and salt scattered across the surface than on their plates. Harry had been in the same year all through school as Dean. The Bewicks had never been the best looking of siblings, but time, alcohol, cigarettes, drugs and toxic anger had made them even uglier...inside and out.

Harry ignored the remark and turned back to Antoni. Dean and Linda never said anything worth listening to. Today would be no exception.

"Take no notice of those idiots," he said to Antoni, who had clearly been wounded by the comment.

Dean was not discouraged. "It's about time someone did something about all the shit around here. The place is overrun with vermin. Bloody foreigners. Well, there's two less of the fuckers to worry about this morning." He chuckled.

"Yeah," Linda contributed. "'Bout time we got rid of the scummy bastards."

"Somebody has definitely got the right idea," Dean continued. "I wonder which waste of space he'll fillet next."

Harry leapt to his feet and turned on them. He saw from the instant look of delight on the Bewicks' faces that they were pleased with his reaction.

"The only scum I know is right in front of me," he pressed on, regardless. "A pair of wasters who've never done a stroke of honest work in their lives."

"You would say that, wouldn't you?" Dean grinned, revealing his small, yellowed teeth. There was dried egg yolk around his mouth. "Sitting there with your Pol friend."

"*Boyfriends*," Linda sneered. "He's as fucking dirty as they are. Worse, even. He shags them."

They both cackled, drawing disgusted stares from the other customers.

"The way I see it, someone is doing Nyemouth a favour. Once they've exterminated the Pols and the Blacks, they can start on some of the queers. Far too many of them around here for my liking."

"I always thought you were an idiot at school," Harry said. "I didn't realise your brain was in its prime back then. Nowadays, you're as stupid as you are ugly — the pair of you."

Several of the other customers laughed and cheered his comments.

Linda's face flushed with indignation. "Well, you're... You're a fucking puff."

Jake Wrangler, the co-owner of the café with his stepsister Lizzie, came out of the kitchen right then. Jack had been on the lifeboat the day before and, together with Harry, had fought to save Niko's life on his boat. His face was a mask of fury. "Your lunch won't be long," he said to Harry, raising a smile for him.

Jake then turned to Dean and Linda. He leaned over the table and lowered his voice, so only those close by could hear. "You two have had enough warnings. Take your prejudices and nasty opinions and get the fuck out. You're not welcome here anymore."

The Bewicks were no longer smiling. "But...but... you can't."

Lizzie appeared at Jake's side. "Oh, we can do a lot more than that. Do as my brother says and get the fuck out that door now or I'll make sure you're barred from every café, bar and shop in the marina."

The Bewicks, realising they were defeated, got begrudgingly to their feet and shuffled around the table to the door. Then Dean turned back. Too stupid to control himself, he directed a tirade of racist and homophobic abuse at Harry, Antoni, Jake and Lizzie.

Harry crossed his arms and glowered at Dean with all the contempt he deserved.

No matter how beautiful this town was, there would always be a current of badness running through it. Yesterday's tragedy should have brought the community together, but the Bewicks were a living example of how fractured it was.

Chapter Seven

Christian smiled softly as he read Harry's message. He'd hoped to hear from him and had made a promise to himself that he would get in touch if there had been no word by mid-afternoon. The tingle of excitement that rippled all through his body was proof the attraction between them was real and his exhausted mind hadn't imagined it at the end of a difficult day.

He keyed in a quick reply.

I'm fine. I hope everything is okay with you, too. Five p.m. sounds good. Let me know a place.

Does it sound too casual? he wondered. The alternative was to send a message that could go too far and come across as gushing and overly dramatic or desperate. *No. Casual is just right. For now.*

He hit Send and put the phone away. There was work to be done.

From the lifeboat station, he could see all the way downriver to where the twin piers stretched out into the sea. The gossip he'd heard earlier proved to be true, and there were indeed police officers working on the south pier. It was too far away for him to see anything other than the minute figures of a forensic team in white coveralls. If he was going to apply journalistic methods to his book research, the pier was the first place to start.

Christian followed the course of the harbour in that direction. A sailboat glided along the river, its gentle wake disturbing the grey mirrored surface of the water. Everything was calm and quiet, a dramatic contrast to the conditions just twenty-four hours earlier.

There were more sailboats and several high-powered yachts and pleasure cruisers moored, and at the end of the dock, Christian realised he could go no farther. A row of ancient holiday homes stood on the bank. Refurbished fisherman's houses, he guessed. The location provided them with an excellent view of the harbour, but there appeared to be no public footpath around them. Christian looked about, wishing he'd bothered to pick up a town map from the hotel reception. Because Nyemouth was relatively small, he'd assumed it would be easy to navigate.

There had to be an access road behind the cottages.

He retraced his route, as far back as The Fisherman's Arms, and found a tourist sign pointing to Pier Street. Now, that sounded promising. He followed the direction into a narrow, cobbled street that seemed to run parallel to the harbour. There were shops, restaurants and bars on either side. Christian guessed they must be listed buildings, as all the fronts were designed in a similar style, in keeping with the old town.

He would have to spend some time researching the history of Nyemouth itself. This must be one of the oldest parts. He already knew from the guidebooks that the port dated as far back as the 1600s, and the stone buildings on this narrow street were most likely from that time.

The path was on an incline, and soon the muscles in his calves ached with the upward trek over uneven cobbles. There were many tourist shops and a lot of small cafes. There was no time to explore in any detail right now. He wanted to get to the pier before the police packed up but would check them out on the route back.

He came upon another sign. To the right, it pointed to a steep set of stone steps – South Bank. The arrow for South Pier pointed straight ahead.

There was something atmospheric, almost gothic, in these ancient streets. He would have to pay them a visit at night and discover just how moody and mysterious it could be. His mind was already busy with scenes of potential danger and intrigue that the setting provoked.

At the end of the shopping street, he found what he assumed to be the back entrances to the holiday cottages and followed the road. At the end, there were two police vans and another two cars. There was still no sight of the pier from this location, but he was clearly on the right trail. He continued on a footpath along the foot of the imposing cliff. Thirty yards on, the path descended towards the pier.

Entry to the pier had been cordoned off by police tape and a uniformed officer kept the public at bay. A crowd of around twenty were idling around, trying to see what was happening farther out, where the forensic team had assembled a tent. Christian spotted a cameraman and journalist, clearly from the local news station, and headed in their direction. The cameraman was busy filming the action on the pier, so he moved in on the journalist, a woman in her mid-thirties with short brown hair. She wore a red puffer jacket over her smart TV suit.

"Hi," he said. "Christian Costner, from the *Manchester Gazette*. Any developments?"

The woman gave him a dismissive glance before turning her attention back to the forensic team. "Manchester? This is a little far from your beat, isn't it?"

"I'm off duty," he said, hoping to win her over with breezy charm. "Here on holiday, in fact. But you know what it's like. Our curiosity is never really switched off."

She looked at him again. "You're not the tourist who was on the boat with the first victim, are you?"

He shook his head. "Afraid not. I only got here last night." A shitty move, but the facts of what he experienced on *The North Star* were not for mass consumption. He owed Niko's family that much.

She sucked her teeth. "Too bad."

"So, who are you with? TV? Radio?"

The woman looked him over, weighing him up, then seemed to relax. "Marie Baxter-Booth. *North-East News*. We're waiting for an update that we can put out on the six o'clock edition, though it looks doubtful. The police are giving nothing away."

"What do you know so far?"

She gestured to the pier. "They seem to think this is where the Jasinski boy was attacked."

"How do they know? And wouldn't any evidence have been washed away by the storm last night?"

"A witness from one of the cottages claims to have seen him walking out this way yesterday afternoon — and that was the last anyone saw of the boy until the boat picked him up. They must have discovered something to have brought the CSI team in. Maybe some blood soaked into the boards before the storm came? Or possibly fibres got caught there. I don't know, but they appear to have something."

As Marie was talking, Christian pressed the advantage. "What about the other guy? The second murder? Are you working on a connection?"

"Too soon to say. My colleague is following that case."

"It seems like such a huge coincidence."

Her lips curled back in a bemused grin. "Anywhere else and I'd say you were right but not here, not in Nyemouth. You've picked a hell of a place for a holiday. This would be right at the bottom of my wish list. I don't know what it is — the town or the people — but there's something off about it. I reported on the Arnie Walker story a couple of summers ago. Then again, last year, when a local businessman tried to kill his ex-husband and his new partner. I was not at all surprised when I got the call out to come here again this morning. This town, I swear to you, attracts bad news."

* * * *

When he had finished at the boat, Harry hurried home to shower and change into fresh clothes, just in time to meet Christian at five o'clock. Christian was having dinner at Dominic Melton's house that night, so Harry suggested he join him at his hotel bar to save time.

Quay Hotel had been a landmark in Nyemouth marina his entire life. An old coaching inn dating back to the eighteenth century, it had been heavily renovated sometime in the 1980s, when the owners had purchased the building at the rear of the property and knocked through to create the hotel. It had been modernised again in 2016 to make it the best accommodation in town. Located at harbour level, its views were not as spectacular as the hotels and guest houses up on the cliffs, but it made up for it in grandeur and history.

The latest makeover was entirely sympathetic to the original architecture, maintaining the old-world charm alongside modern facilities.

Harry reached the hotel exactly at five. As well as the main entrance for residents, there was a street level entry to the ground-floor bar. He went inside and searched for Christian. The bar was large and open, with two fireplaces burning at either end. It was already dark outside, and the lights were on, though they had been dimmed to create a soft, relaxing mood.

Christian was sitting at a table in a bay window that overlooked the river, but the twinkling view appeared to be lost on him. A map of the town was spread out in front of him while he scribbled rapidly across the pages of a notebook. There was also an empty coffee cup at his side.

"This looks interesting," Harry said.

When Christian looked up, took off his glasses and smiled at him, something inside Harry flipped. *What was that?* He couldn't deny he'd been looking forward to seeing him again but hadn't expected such a physical reaction when he did.

Christian looked hot. There was no ignoring the fact. He wore a white shirt, open at the neck. His greying stubble had been trimmed since he'd seen him last night, and his hair was neatly combed with a side part. Those light-grey eyes were magnetic.

Shit, I really do have the hots for him.

"I thought I should get to know my subject," Christian said. "If I'm to base a story here, I need to know the town inside out. And it seems like there is a lot to learn." He closed the notebook and folded the map. "Let me get you a drink. What would you like? Beer? Wine?"

"Just a coffee will be fine. A cappuccino or latte…anything milky."

Their eyes connected as Christian stood and held long enough for their intention to be clear. "I'll be right back."

Christian wore a pair of navy chinos that were snug on the arse. Harry couldn't stop himself from admiring the view as he went to the bar.

Harry sat and tried to calm down. Though his attraction to Christian had developed the day before, he hadn't expected to be quite so into him today. Part of him thought his interest might have fizzled out overnight and he'd discover that he didn't fancy Christian quite so much when they met again, but the opposite was true. The draw was even stronger. Christian was a hottie, no denying that, especially for his age. Harry reproached himself. Why was he so hung up on Christian's age? He couldn't be *that* old. When he'd run into Antoni earlier, he'd remembered there had actually been an eight-year gap between them. It couldn't be much bigger with Christian. *Can it?*

Christian returned, still smiling. "They will bring them over in a minute."

"Thanks. So, is that what you've been doing today?" He gestured to the map and book. "Researching Nyemouth?"

"Yeah," he said, sitting down. "Pretty much wandering around and getting a feel for the place. I lost track of time. It's a fascinating area."

"I guess it is. You don't really notice things like that when you live somewhere your whole life. I probably take it for granted."

"I can't imagine taking anything for granted here. Though, I must say, I'm glad I found you. I can't think of anyone better to help me understand the town than a man who grew up here."

A flush rose over Harry's face. *Oh God, no. Don't start blushing.*

"Well, that is why you chartered the boat," he said as a distraction. "We're good to go out again whenever you're ready. I've got another booking on Friday, but tomorrow and Thursday are free, if they suit you."

"How does the weather look for tomorrow?"

"Not bad. Light winds, no rain, one- to two-metre swells. Nothing to worry about, especially compared to yesterday."

"Okay. Let's go tomorrow."

"I'll call Tom later and let him know. We can maybe head south and show you the coast in that direction."

"Sounds perfect. How is Tom, anyway? Okay, after yesterday, I hope."

"He seemed fine. He helped me with the boat for most of the morning, then left to pick up his son from school. His wife, Susan, got the offer of overtime. It's something she wouldn't have been able to take if we'd been at sea today, so I supposed it worked out for them."

The bartender arrived with their drinks on a tray. Christian swept his book and map onto the empty seat beside him.

"Who is having the decaf?" she asked.

Christian raised his hand and she set one cup in front of him, gave the other to Harry, and laid out the sugar bowls and cream. *Pretty fancy*, Harry thought. The service had improved since the last time he'd been here, and he wondered if there was a new manager in charge.

"Does Tom work with you full-time?" Christian asked.

"No. Unfortunately, I don't have enough work to employ anyone full-time. I wish I could. Things are pretty good from May through to September, weather permitting. My dad helps out a day or two a week over the summer, too, but come this time of year, my work drops right off. I've got just enough jobs booked to keep the boat running through to November, then that's it until spring."

Christian gazed at him thoughtfully. "Then what? How do you survive through the winter?"

"Any way I can. The boat always needs maintenance work, so that takes up a few days. I occasionally help a couple of the fishermen when they need an extra hand. Other than that, I get by doing odd-job work. I'm pretty handy and can turn my attention to most things — decorating, DIY, even a bit of plumbing."

"You can? Impressive. I had to call someone out to fix a leaking tap last month. It cost a bloody fortune."

They both laughed.

"I'm lucky that I also have a small second income," Harry went on. "When my granddad died, he left me his house. It's not far from here, one of the old houses at the foot of the north cliff. It's far too big for my needs, so I converted it into two apartments. I live on the ground floor and let out the upstairs flat to holiday makers during the summer. I did most of the work myself, with a bit of help from my dad. So whatever rental income the flat brings in, I hold back to help me through the down season. It actually does pretty okay over the winter, too, especially at Christmas and New Year."

"Wow. You are a man of many talents."

"I hope you're not planning to use me as a character in your book," he joked. "Or even worse, kill me off."

Christian blew out his cheeks and widened his eyes. "Don't even joke about stuff like that, not after the last day."

"Sorry. Bad taste, I know." He fished a cube of brown sugar out of the bowl and dropped it in his coffee before offering one to Christian. "I ran into my ex, Antoni, this morning," he said as he stirred the coffee and related what Antoni had told him about the Jasinski family.

"Shit. Those poor people. I can't imagine what they must be going through," Christian said when he was finished.

Harry agreed. "But you know how last night we talked about the racist element in Nyemouth? Well, I got to experience some of that first-hand this morning. I was discussing what happened with Antoni when Dean Bewick, an absolute dick I knew at school, and his stupid sister, chimed in with their opinion. It was the kind of crap I would expect from those two—that whoever killed Niko and the other boy had done the town a favour."

"Jesus. It's incredible the bullshit some people will let out of their mouths."

"You've got that right. I've always known that Antoni and his friends had experienced abuse before, but this was the first time I was there to witness it. Those people make me sick. They always have. Thankfully, they are in the minority. Jake, who runs the café, is gay, and his stepsister, Lizzie, is Black, so you can imagine how unwelcome those opinions were. Jake slung their useless arses out, and I'm glad to say all the other customers were appalled."

"You're right. They are the minority. They don't represent the views of everyone. They just make a lot of noise about it. It sounds like the people of Nyemouth proved them wrong today."

Harry experienced another sudden rush when Christian looked at him so tenderly. His eyes were like Nordic pools in the soft light, and his face was possibly the most handsome thing Harry had ever seen. He looked away, confused, and concentrated on his coffee again. He didn't understand these feelings, and each surge was stronger than the last. Was he still messed up over yesterday? Was the old 'sex and death' connection still playing with him?

Harry didn't think so. And if not, it meant he fancied Christian harder and faster than anyone he'd ever known before.

He was determined not to do anything he would regret. Whatever this thing was, he would take his time to process it and not get carried away.

Easier said than done when there is such a hot man sitting inches away from me.

Chapter Eight

"This is me," Harry said, gesturing to the end property in a terrace of four sandstone houses. At the foot of the north cliff, the houses faced directly onto the harbour.

Christian stared, wide-eyed, then laughed. "Wow. Such a long commute to work each morning. How do you manage to get there on time?" He cocked his head towards the boats moored nearby.

Harry's mouth lengthened into a sexy grin, and he gave a modest shrug. "I manage somehow. Most days, anyhow."

"This looks beautiful," Christian said, appraising the property. "I'm jealous. My flat in Manchester has a fantastic view of the alley that runs between the next building and mine."

"You should come in for a look... When you have more time."

Christian was already running a few minutes late for his dinner with Dominic and Arnie. Friends were one of the most important things in life, but just for tonight, he wished he hadn't made plans to see them. After a couple of coffees in the bar, he longed to spend more time with Harry. They could have shared a bottle of wine, some food, and maybe, just maybe, pick up from where they'd left off the previous night.

Standing outside his house with his skin coloured golden by the light cast from the streetlamps, Harry took Christian's breath away. Without thinking, Christian reached across and took his hand, just a gentle touch of their fingers. He tingled with delight when Harry did not pull away.

"I would love to," he said. "Maybe later this week?"

Harry looked straight at him. The pause before he answered was deep, full of unspoken meaning, and then he said, "I'd like that. We can sort out a day. You could come back here for something to eat. I could ask one of the fishermen to keep me something back for dinner."

Christian exhaled, elated. "That's an offer I can't refuse."

Harry nodded and his cheeks darkened in the amber light. He seemed a little bashful. It was so out of character from the confident man of the sea Christian was used to. *Cute. And hot.*

"So, I'll see you at the dock in the morning. Say eight o'clock?"

"I'll be there. I'll bring the coffees."

Harry shook his head. "No. That's my job. All part of the service. Decaf, right?"

"Hey, you know me already."

"I'm learning." He pulled away, moving to his front door. "Have a good night. Say hi to the guys for me."

"I will. Good night."

The path and steps up to the north cliff were steep, winding around hairpin bends. Any other time, Christian might have made hard work of it, but tonight, he ascended in an effortless stride. His forty-two-year-old body felt light, and more agile than it had at twenty-one. He'd bought two bottles of wine at the hotel and they clinked together in the bag as he bounced up the steps. He paused at the top to inhale the fresh air, drawing it deep into his lungs. He exhaled, taking in the view from the cliff top.

Was there a more beautiful place in the whole world? Not this evening.

He hadn't appreciated from below how steep the valley Nyemouth nestled in was. The river was a black mirror, so far down, reflecting the lights of the town on its near-perfect surface. It was hard to grasp how wild the conditions had been twenty-four hours earlier. The winds had been so severe that he doubted he would have been able to stand on the spot where he was now without being blown over.

The two lighthouses at the ends of each pier flashed their gentle warning out to sea, but there was no danger tonight. For one moment, Christian could almost forget what had happened since he had arrived here — but not for long. His gaze was drawn across the water, to the south pier. It was too far to make out much detail, but it looked as though the police forensic unit had gone. The journalist in him couldn't help wondering what they had discovered, if anything. It still seemed likely that the storm would have carried away all evidence.

With a sigh, he turned away from the cliff and set off in search of Dominic's house.

It wasn't hard to find. Cliff House stood out on the point, even at night. A grand old stone building, it had to be at least two-hundred years old.

Christian rang the bell. There was a flash of movement through the frosted glass and the door was answered by a young boy, who looked around twelve but tall for his age. He was unseasonably dressed in a Spider-Man T-shirt and shorts, with bare feet.

"Hi," the boy said. "They're waiting for you in the kitchen. Come through."

"You must be AJ," he said, stepping inside and closing the door behind him.

The boy smiled, and it struck Christian just how much the young man looked like his famous father, Arnie. He was already shooting up to match his father's huge frame. He had the same dark-blond hair and pale blue eyes. "Yeah, I am. Have you recovered from your trip yesterday? I was watching. I saw your boat coming in from the window upstairs. I can see all the way out from up there." His eyes were wide with child-like ghoulish excitement.

Christian widened his stance and made an exaggerated show of steading himself. "I think I've just about got used to dry land again."

"It did look rough. Were you worried the boat might capsize?"

He laughed. "I never even thought of it. But now you've put the idea in my head…"

"Oh, that hardly ever happens," AJ said matter-of-factly. "We've lived here for over two years now and I've never seen it. Neither has Dominic, and he's been here for much longer."

"Now, I'm reassured," he said.

AJ led him through the house to a large open-plan kitchen and dining room. "Here they are," he said.

Dominic was busy at the stove. Like AJ, he was barefoot, in knee length denim shorts and a dark polo shirt, with an apron tied around him. He was busy stirring something in a pot. He grinned at Christian over his shoulder. "Hey. Won't be a minute."

Arnie, similarly dressed in shorts and a light shirt, closed the fridge door. Christian realised how warm the house was. He would hate to have these guys' fuel bill. Though they had only met once before, Arnie came in and greeted him with a friendly hug. Christian had always considered himself tall at six-one, but he felt dwarfed by Dominic's hunky husband. As Dominic was also a good few inches shorter than Christian, they were a mismatched and yet perfectly suited pair.

"Great to see you again," Arnie said. "I'm so glad Dominic talked you into visiting. Though I bet you didn't expect our little town to be quite so eventful, eh?"

"That's no understatement." Christian raised his bag of wine bottles. "I wasn't sure what you guys were into, so I got a red and a white."

"We drink anything," Dominic said, wiping his hands on his apron and coming over for another welcome hug.

"Ha ha. I thought as much, but didn't like to presume."

"Fancy a cocktail before dinner?" Arnie asked, returning to the fridge.

"What's on offer?"

"Well, I'm having a martini, but Dominic's on beer. So take your pick—or we can open some wine."

"A martini sounds great. Thank you."

Christian took in the dining table. It had been covered with a red table cloth and set with three place mats, chargers, formal cutlery placements, wine glasses and a water jug. There were fresh flowers, candles and tealights on the table.

"Hey, I didn't know you were going to all this trouble."

"I set the table," AJ told him.

"But there's only three places."

"I had pizza earlier. I'm not going to eat *that* stuff." He grimaced and pointed at Dominic stirring the pot.

"Don't worry," Arnie said. "We only got the fancy plates out because we hardly ever have an opportunity otherwise. They were wedding presents, and we feel bad for not using them. As you can see," he spread his arms to show off his casual attire, "we haven't made as much of an effort with ourselves."

AJ looked bored with the adults. "Dad, can I watch an episode of *Cobra Kai*?"

Arnie cocked an eyebrow. "Nice try. No way. You know it's too old for you. You can watch one episode of *Superman and Lois* then bed. Okay?"

The boy smiled, knowing he'd been foxed, and left the kitchen.

"He's a typical kid," Arnie said. "Always wanting to watch the stuff he shouldn't."

"I used to be into all the things I shouldn't have at that age," Christian admitted. "The *Alien* movies were my favourites. I don't think it did me much harm."

"Oh, I know I'm fighting a losing battle. He'll win me over soon enough. I just want him to hang onto the last bit of childhood for as long as possible. He'll have the rest of his life for the grown-up stuff."

Dominic returned to the stove. "How about you, Christian? Have you ever had any urge to start a family?"

He rolled his eyes. "I haven't got a paternal bone in my body. Don't get me wrong. I love being the eccentric gay uncle. I have a brother and a sister and between them I have two nieces and a nephew, but short visits are about all I have the patience for. I love the quiet when they go home, too."

Arnie chuckled. "That's what bedtime is for. A couple of precious hours of daddy time, though we're often too tired to appreciate it."

"Yeah," Dominic agreed. "Falling asleep in front of the TV is a common event for us. There must be a hundred movies I've only ever seen the first half hour of."

Their soft protests did not fool Christian. It was clear how much these guys adored each other and what a happy household this was.

Arnie got busy with a cocktail shaker. Christian watched as he added vodka and vermouth — all by eye, there were no measurements — before ladling in crushed ice. He put on the lid and gave it a vigorous shake before straining it into two martini glasses. "More wedding presents," he explained. For the last touch, he used a fruit knife to peel two slivers of rind off a lemon and dropped them in.

Christian took a sip. The hit of alcohol was instant, strong and delicious. Despite no measures, Arnie had got the blend of vodka and vermouth just right. The twist of lemon gave a hint of freshness. "Perfect. And if you ever tire of acting, you should think about opening a cocktail bar."

Arnie's eyes sparkled. "Now *that* is a great suggestion. A nice wine and cocktail bar down there on the waterfront."

Dominic gave a good-natured groan. "Please don't give him ideas like that." He removed his apron. "Okay, this needs about forty minutes then to stand for another fifteen. How about we sit down and finish these drinks then I'll serve the starters?"

"There are starters? Guys, please, I wasn't expecting any of this."

Arnie raised a hand. "We already told you we don't entertain much. Humour us."

Dominic gestured to a comfortable seating area in front of two closed French doors. Lights outside illuminated a resplendent patio and garden. They sat on two cream leather sofas, Dominic and Arnie side by side, with Christian facing them across a low coffee table.

"You have a lovely home," he remarked.

"We can't take much of the credit," Arnie said. "I started out renting this place and loved it so much we bought it as it was, furniture and all. It's practically the same as it was the day when I moved in. Apart from a fresh coat of paint now and then, I wouldn't change a thing."

"I can see why. It's like something out of a lifestyle magazine. Congratulations, guys." He raised his glass in a celebratory gesture.

Dominic lounged back with his beer and popped his feet up on the fancy coffee table. "So, how has your day been? Are you still okay after yesterday?"

"I'm fine, really. Once or twice, I've been hit with a rush of emotions as what happened on the boat comes flooding back, but I've kept it in check. I've been busy."

He told them about his research and exploration of the town.

"Well," Dominic said when he had finished, "I've heard a little news, if you care to hear it. No, I should clarify that. I've heard *gossip*. Not the same thing at all."

Arnie turned to look at his husband. "And I wonder where you picked that up. Jacob?"

Dominic chuckled. "Got it in one. There's nothing much that goes on in Nyemouth that old guys don't hear about."

"He has eyes and ears all over the place," Arnie laughed.

"He claims he doesn't ask about any of it. That people just *tell* him all this stuff."

"He's like Nyemouth's very own Miss Marple."

Christian sipped the martini. "Well, as I found out today, there is no concrete news, so you might as well fill me in on the gossip."

Dominic picked at the label on his beer bottle. "Do you know much about the second victim?"

"Not a lot. Just that he worked at a local supermarket."

"Who was he?" Arnie asked.

"Ike. Ike Meeker."

"Do we know him?"

"Not personally. I've seen him around. Maybe you have, too. If you saw a photo, you might recognise him. So, apparently, he was found by his mother early last night."

"Oh, God," Arnie said. "The poor woman. That's the worst thing that could happen to any parent."

"Ike has his own place, but his mother still does his washing and cooking. All that stuff. I gather she was dropping something off when she found him. The neighbours heard her screaming for help. The details are pretty sketchy. I'm not sure what I believe. I think there's so much gossip flying about that people are getting Niko and Ike mixed up anyway."

"Did the guys know each other?" Christian asked.

Dominic shrugged. "Probably. It's a small town. Everybody knows somebody, but I don't know if it went any deeper than that. There's talk that Ike's murder might have been a botched burglary. Some of his things are missing—laptop, phone, you know, the usual stuff that thieves go for. There's a train of thought that he came home from work and caught a burglar doing the place over."

"It sounds extreme but not impossible," Christian said. "Though most thieves do a runner as soon as they're disturbed. They rarely hang around and fight."

"A lot of other people think there's a serial killer on the loose, like Jason or Michael Myers. You know, someone who attacks people at random. It's pretty dumb, but it strikes me as wishful thinking. These folk get off on the excitement of talking about things like that, but it's hardly going to be true. Is it?"

Arnie gave Dominic a playful nudge. "Short memory, much?"

"This isn't the same. You had a stalker. These are just two random attacks that people want to be connected. They thrive on the drama of it."

"What else are they saying? You said there was gossip," Christian reminded him.

"A lot of crap, really. None of it will be true."

"And don't forget we're writers. We listen to everything."

"Fair point," Dominic said. "So, I take it you've heard of these sites like OnlyFans and JustFor.Fans?"

"Sure?"

"Fill me in," Arnie said. And when Christian and Dominic shot him sceptical looks, "What? Look... I know it's something to do with sex, but I don't know what it is."

Dominic laughed. "It's like an app, or a website or something. People upload sexy pictures and videos of themselves and charge a fee for others to look at them."

"Most of them are subscription services," Christian told him. "Fans pay a monthly fee to access someone's exclusive content."

"Porn?" Arnie asked.

"Some would insist not. There are other types of content on those sites, but I'd hazard a guess that the majority of what users pay for is the sex stuff. What does it have to do with the murders?"

"It doesn't," Dominic said. "But Jacob heard a rumour that Niko had posted videos to some of those sites."

"For fuck's sake." Arnie scowled. "Is that really what people are talking about? The poor kid is dead, his family is devastated and they're trying to smear his reputation. What does it matter? Do they think he had it coming because he posted a few dick pics? Talk about victim blaming."

Dominic raised his hands. "Don't shoot the messenger. I'm just telling you what I heard."

Arnie groaned. "You know, sometimes I think this place hasn't moved on at all. It's the same small-minded town I grew up in. Ugh. People can be awful."

"*Some* people," Dominic corrected. "A small minority."

"Let's change the subject, anyway," Christian suggested. "It's a bit grim for the dinner table, especially when you've gone to so much trouble."

Arnie told him to take a seat at the table while he opened the wine. Dominic had prepared a starter of macaroni and crab, presented in small ramekins with a side salad and roasted cherry tomatoes. Christian leaned in and inhaled the delicious aroma as it steamed on the plate.

"You made this? It's incredible."

"Enjoy."

The food was so good that they devoured it in complete silence. "Huge compliments to the chef. Thank you," Christian said when they had finished.

"You're welcome," Dominic said, wiping his lips with a linen napkin.

After a moment, Christian realised that the guys were watching him across the table, mischievous smiles on their faces.

"What?" he asked.

They exchanged cunning glances before Dominic asked, "How are you getting on with the lovely Harry?"

"Oh, God, really?"

"Come on," Arnie said over the top of his wine glass. "We want to know."

"What can I say?" Christian laughed, feeling the heat colour his face. "He's nice."

"Nice? I think you can do better than that. I thought you said you were a writer."

He sat back in his chair and blew out his cheeks. "Harry seems like a lovely guy. More than lovely. Actually, I met him for a coffee just before I came here."

The couple exchanged another knowing look.

"Told you," Arnie said.

"Told him what?" Christian asked.

"We speculated on why you were late," Dominic said. "Harry was at the top of our list."

Christian stared at them, open-mouthed. "I wasn't that late."

"But you're usually punctual to fault."

He laughed. "Okay. You got me."

"So come on," Arnie pressed. "What comes after coffee?"

"We'll have to see. We're going out in the boat again tomorrow, so that's what happens next."

"You're right," Dominic said. "Harry is a lovely guy. I think you should go for it. Whatever *it* is?"

"We'll see."

"Why not? What's the problem?"

Christian took solace in the wine before answering, "I feel like I'm old enough to be his father."

They both laughed. "Hardly. He's not a boy, you know. There's maybe ten, twelve years between you. Besides, Harry is an old soul. He has been for as long as I've known him. When other guys his age were out partying and getting drunk, he used to go home early so he could take the boat out in the morning."

"Anyway, I reckon once you're over twenty-five there's no such thing as an age gap," Arnie said. "Don't let something so trivial put you off."

"Guys, stop. I only met the poor bloke yesterday. We barely know each other. Let's just figure this out for ourselves, eh?" Christian took another gulp of wine, masking his emotions. The truth was, he couldn't wait to see Harry again in the morning.

He just wasn't ready to admit it.

Not yet.

Chapter Nine

Harry was waiting on the deck of *The North Star* by seven-thirty the next morning. He had a feeling Christian would be early and wanted to be ready for him. Was it really a hunch or just wishful thinking on his part? Though he'd slept well enough last night, his dreams had been filled with the charismatic journalist. He couldn't remember many of the details when he shook himself awake, other than a few lingering images, but he'd got out of bed feeling hornier than he had been in months.

The fuzzy passion of his dreams lingered, and he couldn't wait to see Christian again. He glanced along the harbour with breathless anticipation.

Christian appeared at ten-to-eight. The morning had dawned unseasonably warm, and he carried his jacket over his arm. He wore jeans and a light-grey sweater, which skimmed the perfect shape of his chest and torso. Harry's pulse quickened as he approached the edge of the dock.

This is escalating fast. Harry had found Christian mildly attractive on Monday. Now, a few hot dreams later, he was the sexiest man he'd ever seen.

"Morning," he beamed. "Take care coming down that ladder. It's slippery."

Christian flung his legs over the edge of the quay and scuttled down to the boat, giving Harry a nice view of his juicy butt. "Morning to you, too."

Harry passed him a cup of takeaway coffee and a paper bag. "I didn't know if you'd have had time for breakfast, so I got you a bacon roll."

Christian's smile brightened further. "Thanks very much. As it happens, I haven't. I had one too many drinks with Dominic and Arnie last night, and I felt a little fragile when I first got up. I couldn't face food straight away."

"Oh. Are you okay to go to sea? We can hold off a couple of hours if you need time to pull yourself together."

"I'm fine. It was just a heavy head — nothing a couple of painkillers couldn't fix." He took the lid off the coffee cup and sipped. "Thanks for breakfast."

"All part of the service." Harry watched with delight as Christian tore into the paper wrapper and took a bite of the sandwich. He liked guys with good appetites. He'd once dated a man who had been obsessed with his gym routine and the nutritional value of everything he ate and drank — a real pain in the arse whenever they went out together. It was good to see Christian eat with such obvious pleasure. "I picked up a couple of salad boxes for lunch, too. The weather looks set to hold, so we can stay out for as long as you'd like today — even make up some of the time we lost on Monday."

Christian looked beyond Harry, into the cabin. He swallowed and said, "Are we waiting for Tom? Or is he down below?"

Harry shook his head. "He's not coming. He texted late last night to say he had childcare problems. Don't worry. We'll be fine without him. I usually bring him along to deal with my clients, but seeing as it's just you today, I'm sure I can manage."

He caught the sparkle in Christian's eyes, the upward turn of a smile on his wide lips. "I'm sure you can. You've already got off to a good start."

Their eyes lingered a moment before Harry untied one of the mooring ropes. "Your lifejacket's in the cabin there. Slip it on, and we'll get going."

Christian brushed past him, his chest grazing Harry's shoulder. The contact had to be deliberate. It sent a thrill right through him.

"Yes, captain. I'll put myself in your capable hands."

Harry couldn't keep the grin from his face as he undid the ropes and returned to the cabin. Christian fastened the straps of the lifejacket around him, and Harry started the engine.

"Is there anything you'd especially like to see?" He edged the vessel out into the river and turned her around to face the harbour exit. Most of the fishing boats were already out, and he had a clear run towards the piers.

"How about heading in the opposite direction to the other day?"

"Yep. No problem."

Harry's gaze drifted to the south bank and pier as they glided past. A couple of anglers were fishing off the end, but there was no sign of the police unit that had been stationed there yesterday.

"Any further news?" Christian asked, following the direction of his eyes.

Harry shook his head, turning his attention back to the river ahead. "Not that I've heard. Idle speculation in the café this morning, but nothing more than that. It will keep them talking for a few days until something else takes their attention."

Christian moved closer, standing right behind him at the wheel. "I get the impression that while you love this town, you don't have a high opinion of many of the residents."

Harry laughed. "You've quite observant. I guess that's why you're a reporter. You're also right. All this small-town gossip and bitching gets on my tits. Some of these folks literally have nothing better to do than put others down. Their minds are narrower than the Nye Valley. They were born here, they'll die here and they'll never aspire to do anything else."

"But you've been here your whole life, too. Doesn't that hypothesis apply to you also?"

As they left the protection of the harbour, the sea was remarkably calm. The boat rolled gently in the swell but was nothing to worry about. The most fair-weather sailors would be content with today's conditions.

"Guilty," he said. "But I'm not one of those people. I know Nyemouth is not the be-all and end-all. It's a nice place, but it has its problems. It's no better than anywhere else. We've got some fantastic people living here and some real arseholes. It just happens to have a nice coastal location. But the people who do the moaning and bitching don't even appreciate that. They're too damn lazy to walk up onto the cliff tops or along the beach. It would never occur to most of them to get out of town and explore the moors. They just sit on their arses and complain about the tourists. They infuriate me at times."

He heard Christian chuckle behind him. "Why don't you tell me how you really feel?"

Harry sighed. "Sorry. I'll get down off my high horse." He flashed a smile over his shoulder. "We're about to turn south. There are some amazing views all along this section of the coast. So, just over there is the south cliff. You'll find some excellent walking trails along both cliff tops if you fancy exploring the area by land rather than sea. Shout out if you see anything you want a closer look at. The coast is pretty rugged, but there are a few places where I can get the boat near to the shore."

Harry focused on the wheel and the route ahead, leaving Christian in peace to take photographs and scribble in his notebook. The eroticism of his dreams lingered, and he fought hard to put them aside. There was no point dwelling on it. He couldn't deny that he found Christian increasingly attractive, but in a few days from now, he would leave Nyemouth and they would likely not see each other again. With the wide horizon in front of him, Harry recognised his fancy for what it was…a crush, nothing more meaningful than that. It would run its course in another day or so, and that would be the end of it.

Time passed quickly at sea. The mild weather improved as the morning went on and soon they enjoyed clear skies and perfect conditions. Motoring along the coast, past fishing boats and small towns, answering Christian's questions, Harry was surprised when he checked his watch and discovered it had gone twelve o'clock. They would have to turn back soon.

"Are you hungry?" he asked.

Christian put down his camera. "Actually, yes. I didn't expect to be, especially after your generous breakfast."

"It's the sea air," Harry told him. "It gives everyone an appetite."

"Unless they're sick," Christian grinned.

"Well, yes, there's always a risk of that. But you look fresh enough to me."

"I feel great."

"That's what I want to hear."

Harry slowly turned the boat around and headed farther out to sea. Once he was satisfied that they were well clear of the fishing nets, he cut the engine and let the boat idle in the swell. They could safely drift for an hour or so out here without any risk. On a regular trip, he would have Tom to take care of their lunches, but today he would have to deal with it himself.

He pointed at a thermos in the wheelhouse. "There's coffee in there if you want something hot. It won't taste as good as the stuff this morning, but it's better than the instant stuff I've got onboard. I forgot to shop this week and stock up on the ground stuff."

"You've had other things on your mind," Christian said. "The thermos is fine."

"I'll be right back," he said, hovering over the hatch to the lower deck. "Can I fetch you a cold drink? There's cola, beer, water."

"Water will be fine. Thank you."

Harry scooted below and grabbed two bottles of water and the salad boxes he'd bought earlier from the fridge. Christian was sitting on the bench in the stern, drinking coffee from an old mug, when he climbed back up. The midday sun caught the strong angles of his face, making him look even more handsome than ever. Harry's pulse quickened.

Steady. This is only a crush, remember? You'll get over it.

He crossed the deck and sat beside him. "I've got roast chicken or prawns. Which do you prefer?" he asked, holding up the salads.

"I'm fine with either. Chicken, I guess."

Harry handed him the box, together with the water and a fork. "Enjoy."

Christian opened the lid, exposing the deliciously packed content. "Wow. This looks good."

"Jake puts them up at the Seagull. If you haven't already eaten there, you should treat yourself. It would be a shame to miss out."

"Jake is the guy from the lifeboat, right? The one who came onboard for Niko."

"That's him. He runs the café with his stepsister. They prepare everything themselves daily. It's my favourite place in town, really—for casual eating, I mean. There are a couple of fancy restaurants if you're looking for something more formal, and most of the pubs do great food, too. We're spoiled for choice, really."

"It would appear so." Christian speared a piece of chicken and lettuce with his fork.

They ate in silence for a few minutes, both of them obviously enjoying their lunch. The boat barely moved, just a gentle dip from side to side. Harry savoured the warmth of the sun on his face and neck. There would not be many more days like this until spring.

"So, do you think you got what you came for?" he asked after a while. Christian gave a quizzical look.

"The trips along the coast. Did you get what you needed for your book?"

"Oh." Christian put the empty lunch box on the deck and secured it with his foot. "Yeah. Well, it was never anything as specific as that. I came looking for inspiration, to spark a few ideas—and I got plenty of those. I don't know how they will fit into my next book. That might not come to me for a little while yet, but I know for certain Nyemouth and this whole coastal area will make a fantastic setting."

Harry nodded. "I don't know how you do it. Dominic, either. Coming up with all those stories. I've never been creative in that way. I've always been more practical. Even at school, I was shockingly bad at literature and art but got good grades in geography and history."

Christian turned on the bench to look at him. "I admire someone as practical as you are, how you run and maintain this boat. And last night, when you told me you'd done all the work on the house yourself, that was bloody impressive. I can't do any of that stuff. Plumbing, electrics, decorating... I always need someone to do it for me."

Now Harry chuckled. "I guess not everyone can be good at everything."

"The world would be boring if we were."

"And you're keeping plumbers in work, if nothing else."

"Shady. But you have a good point." Christian gave Harry's thigh a playful slap.

The touch sent electricity all through his body and his cock hardened.

Shit. He was hornier than he'd thought. He shifted position and tried to hide it.

Christian seemed to realise the reaction he had caused. The smile turned serious, and he stared deep into Harry's eyes. For the longest moment neither of them spoke, then Christian placed his hand back on Harry's leg, higher than before. The tip of his thumb grazed Harry's groin.

"Is this all right?" he asked.

Harry swallowed. "More than all right."

Encouraged, Christian squeezed the muscle of his inner thigh. There was no controlling it now. Harry's cock was rock hard.

"It seems we've been building to this moment for a long time," Christian murmured.

They had only known each of three days, but there was a truth to what he'd said. After everything they'd been through, it felt like much longer.

Harry couldn't think of a reply. He didn't need to. Christian leaned closer and pressed his lips to his. Harry couldn't deny this was what he'd been waiting for. He opened his mouth and slid their tongues together. Christian put his other hand on the back of Harry's head and drew him deeper into the kiss.

They broke apart, both grinning, their foreheads touching, breathing heavily.

"I dreamt about this last night," Christian admitted.

"You did? So did I. Well, not exactly like this, but I dreamt about you a lot."

"It seems like we're in tune."

"Must be."

"Let me show you how my dream went." Christian gave him another light kiss on the lips before sliding from the bench to the deck.

He ran both of his hands up Harry's inner thighs. Harry's entire body shuddered at the touch. It was years since he'd experienced the electric touch of a stranger. When he was with Antoni, the sex had been familiar and repetitive—two men who knew each well and who had no surprises left. There had been no one else since they had split. Now today, this hot older man was on his knees in front of him, touching him intimately. Harry trembled with excitement.

Christian reached his groin and drew his fingers across the hardness, outlining the shape of his cock that was leaning to the left inside his jeans. Christian let out a moan of satisfaction. He raised his eyes to Harry's, and there was a wide grin spread across his face. He deftly undid Harry's belt and unfastened his jeans.

"Lift up a moment," Christian instructed.

Harry raised his butt from the bench and Christian pulled down his jeans and underpants in one fluid movement, hauling them all the way to his ankles.

"Now, isn't that better?" Christian said, gazing at his cock.

Harry sat back down and widened his thighs. The temperate air was a pleasant surprise on his hot balls and bare arse. In the years he'd been at sea, he'd never been exposed like this.

Christian had his hands on Harry's thighs again, and his eyes were fixed on his cock.

"Is everything all right?" Harry asked. He knew he had a decent cock, with good length and girth, but it didn't stop the flashes of insecurity whenever he revealed it to a new partner.

"Perfect. It's a thing of beauty. I just wanted a moment to admire it."

He gave a self-conscious laugh, part pleased and part embarrassed. "That must be your artistic side talking again."

"I know a good thing when I see it."

He took Harry's balls in the palm of his hand, cupping them and gently juggling. Harry shuddered all over again, noticing the gooseflesh as it prickled on his bare thighs, the hairs raising. His cock was so hard now that it felt ready to burst. The juicy tip poked through the glistening folds of his foreskin and pre-cum oozed down the shaft.

Christian leaned forward and slithered his tongue along the underside, licking the overflowing fluid.

Harry took an involuntary gasp of breath, his knees jerking upwards. Undeterred, Christian ran his tongue all the way to the tip, swirling it around the sensitive foreskin and glans. *Good God.* Harry gripped the bench with both hands. The featherlight touch of Christian's tongue caused reactions all over his body. The pleasure was beyond exquisite.

His grip tightened further when Christian opened his mouth and enveloped him with hot, wet pressure.

"Shit!" It was like being a virgin again and experiencing a blow job for the first time. The sensations drove him insane.

Christian couldn't fail to realise the reactions he was causing. Harry gasped, trembled and squirmed as he worked him with his mouth, grazing his tongue along the underside of his dick, applying just the right amount of suction, slowly moving his head back and forth. His hands stayed planted on Harry's thighs, and he pleasured him with just his mouth, drawing him closer to release. Harry's balls tingled and drew tighter in their sac. He knew he was close, but Christian kept him on the edge as the pleasure in his nuts intensified.

"Oh, God," he cried at last. "I'm gonna... I'm gonna..."

Even when the climax was inevitable and he knew it could not be stopped, he teetered on the verge for an age. Then it came — an incredible rush that caused his knees to tremble and his stomach to quiver as it released. Christian didn't withdraw, either. He kept Harry's cock in his mouth as the cum pumped and pumped, seeming to swallow it all.

"Whoa," Harry gasped then laughed when he was done. "Oh my God. Man, what did you just do to me?"

Christian finally released his hold, sitting back on his knees. He licked his lips. "Only what I've been thinking about since I got out of bed this morning."

"Seriously?"

"I wouldn't joke about a thing like this," he said, caressing Harry's softening cock. "I dreamt last night that I sucked you off on this boat — and now the dream has come true."

"What else did you dream about?" he asked with a cheeky grin.

"Oh, lots of things. And I'm hoping that all my dreams come true."

Chapter Ten

At six-thirty that evening, Christian waited for Harry in the hotel bar. He nursed a lemon-and-lime-flavoured gin and tonic and couldn't keep the grin off his face as he sipped. They had returned to the harbour around five. Christian hadn't wanted the day to end and suspected Harry felt the same.

"How about I repay your generosity?" he'd said. "You provided my breakfast and lunch. I'd like to return the favour."

"I think you did that already," Harry had replied with a twinkle in his eyes.

"I mean dinner…tonight."

Christian's time in Nyemouth was limited, and he didn't want to waste a moment.

He'd bounded back to the hotel with the lightest of steps, like he was walking on air. Giving Harry a blow job on the boat was the most impulsive thing he could remember doing…ever. What a time to surrender to his instincts. He was still on a high from that rush. If he concentrated, he could summon the taste of Harry's cock and the rich scent of his groin.

He smiled again.

When he'd returned to the hotel, he had run a bath and luxuriated in the tub, listening to the busy sounds in the harbour below and thinking about Harry. Today was supposed to be a research trip for his book, but Christian had given little thought to his fledgling project. The investigations into the murders had also been pushed to the back of his mind, a concern for another day. Being alone with Harry on board the boat had reduced all other problems to nothing.

After his bath, he'd taken his time preparing for their date. He had trimmed his beard to a tidy stubble and put on his favourite underpants. He teamed his beige chinos with a pale blue, open-neck shirt and a pair of tan brogues. He hadn't bothered with a jacket. He had no intention of leaving the hotel that night, and if he did, he could always come back to the room to collect it.

The bar had been busy with early evening diners, but he secured a cosy booth at the back of the room, where they could relax in comfort and privacy. As he sipped his gin, he kept a slightly nervous eye on the door. He didn't think Harry would stand him up, not after the connection they'd made that afternoon, but insecurity was as deep at forty-two as it had been at seventeen.

Christian stifled a yawn. What a great day it had been. Harry had warned him that fresh air worked up an appetite, but he also suspected it had worn him out. He would need all his energy if the evening was to play out the way he hoped.

Harry arrived a few minutes later, and Christian's fatigue vanished in a second.

Oh my God, he's gorgeous.

Harry had also freshened up. He wore jeans and a pristine white T-shirt beneath a black jacket. His dark-blond hair had a damp, just-out-of-the-shower look about it. He stood in the doorway, glancing around. Christian stood and waved him over. Harry's smile when he spotted him illuminated the entire pub.

"Hey." They greeted each other.

There was a rosy flush to Harry's cheeks that was utterly adorable.

"Did you get everything done?" he asked. Harry had been busy finishing off work on the boat when he'd left him earlier.

"Yeah. All good. I don't have another charter until Friday, so I wanted to get everything secure before I left. I need to refuel at some point tomorrow and stock up on supplies, but that should be about it."

"Are you hungry yet? Want me to get us menus?"

"Not really. It's still a little early for me. I'd love a drink, though."

Christian went to the bar and got a beer for Harry and another gin for himself. When he returned to the booth, Harry had taken his jacket off. Christian couldn't miss the firm shape of his torso in the white T-shirt and the dark, delicious shadows of his nipples. A tuft of dark-blond hair peeked over the collar.

"What are you grinning at?" Harry asked as he sat back down, an infectious grin on his own face.

"I've been smiling nonstop since lunchtime, in case you hadn't noticed."

The flush in his cheeks intensified. "Yeah. *That* was pretty special." He lowered his voice. "I haven't come like that since...well, ever."

Christian sat back. "A hot young man like you. Really? That's hard to believe. I imagine you have to fight men off everywhere you go."

He shook his head and sipped the beer. "Nah. Not in this town."

"Don't you go out of Nyemouth? There must be gay bars up in Newcastle, somewhere you can meet other guys."

"Oh, there are, but they're not for me. I can't be bothered with all that posing and effort. I've only been out there a few times, but I didn't like it. No one talks to anyone unless they already know them. It's hard to get noticed unless you're a regular."

Christian nodded agreement. "It's like that most places now. The only way to catch the attention of a man across the room is to find his Grindr profile and message him."

"Right. And I don't go in for those dating apps and stuff. I've been on them three or four times, and it was a waste of time. I don't know what most of those lads are even looking for, but I wasn't it."

"Then they must be blind...or stupid."

"No, I was the stupid one for even trying. In case you hadn't noticed, I'm not one of those regular gays."

What a surprise to hear him talk like this. Until now, all Christian had seen of Harry was the strong-willed, confident seafarer. Out on the boat, nothing phased him. What a difference to see him in a more unguarded frame of mind.

"So, when were you last in a relationship?" Christian asked.

Harry widened his eyes.

"Sorry." Christian raised his hands. "That's the journalist in me. I'm so used to asking questions that I don't know when to stop. Ignore me. I withdraw it."

"No, it's fine. It's just so rare to talk to someone like this. I'm not used to it." He took another sip. "Antoni was my last boyfriend. I told you about him yesterday—the Polish guy who got abuse from our local fuckwits. We were together for nearly three years. He's a lovely man, but we just didn't make it to the next level. Know what I mean? We're still good friends and I hope we always will be, but the romance hadn't been there for a long time when we split up. If anything, things are better between us now, because we get to be friends without the problems that come with being a couple."

Christian couldn't imagine anyone involved with Harry being so dumb as to let the sexual side of the relationship fizzle out. "And there's been no one since?"

He shook his head. "What about you? Manchester has a massive gay scene, doesn't it? You must see plenty of action."

He almost choked on his gin. As he recovered, he said, "You know all those things you said you hate about Newcastle? Well, imagine that multiplied by a hundred. That's what it's like. All the guys I've met these last few years have been the same. They don't want to commit to anything meaningful. They want to keep their options open, hoping there's someone better around the corner—or rather, one DM away. I can't be bothered with all that shit."

Harry grimaced. "That sounds horrendous. So, there's been no one for you, either?"

"I met a guy last Christmas. Dan, he's called—a TV researcher, the same age as me. We had a lot of things in common. We liked the same movies, music, food. I thought I had finally met somebody serious. But after five months, I found out Dan had been sleeping around and using apps the whole time we were seeing each other. So, that was the end of Dan. I'd had enough of shallow, superficial men." He laughed uncontrollably.

"What's so funny? It doesn't sound amusing to me."

He recovered his composure. "I'm laughing at the irony. Here I am slagging off those superficial guys, when just this afternoon I gave a blow job on a boat to a sexy man I met for the first time on Monday."

Now Harry laughed. He put his elbows on the table, leaned forward, and lowered his voice. "I'm not going to complain about that. It was the best."

Christian leaned in, too, breathing in the fresh, soapy scent of his skin and hair. "I can't take all the credit. I had the very best material to work with." Beneath the table, he pressed his knee between Harry's thighs.

"It's not really fair, though," Harry said.

"In what way?"

"Well, you made me come harder than I ever have in my life. But I didn't get a chance to return the favour."

Christian shifted in the seat. His dick was uncomfortably hard in his pants. If they weren't in a busy pub, he'd have crawled under the table and taken his fill of that beautiful cock all over again.

"If you're not hungry yet, how about we go up to my room for a while?"

Harry's eyes shone with delight and hunger. He knocked off the rest of his beer. "Show me the way."

Chapter Eleven

Christian's fingers trembled as he pulled his room card from his wallet and swiped the lock. It was strange, at his age, to feel the butterflies of young passion flutter through him. He stepped inside and clicked the switch for the table and bedside lights, bathing the room in their warm glow. Harry followed, shutting the door.

"Nice," Harry said. "I've always wondered what the bedrooms were like in this place."

Christian crossed to the windows and closed the curtains. The nearest properties were across the river and there was no direct line of sight, but a lifetime of close city dwelling had conditioned him to privacy.

Before he turned around, Harry was right behind him. He gripped Christian's butt in both hands and put his chin on his shoulder. His breath was hot against Christian's ear when he spoke.

"I've been wanting to get my hands on this all day." He flicked Christian's earlobe with his tongue.

Christian shivered, pressing his arse into Harry's palms. "What took you so long?"

Harry nuzzled the hollow of his neck. His beard was soft and glossy against his skin. "I'm a little reserved about things like that."

"I'm glad you've overcome that problem," Christian said, tipping his head back to give unrestricted access to this throat.

Harry moved his hands around Christian's waist and pressed his hips against his buttocks. The bulge of his cock fit into the cleft, and Christian swayed gently, relishing the heat and hardness of Harry's erection. He knew what to expect, having already had the pleasure of Harry's cock in his mouth, but Christian wanted him in many more ways than that.

He raised a hand behind him, stroking the side of Harry's face. "I want you to fuck me," he drawled.

"Mm-m," Harry pressed kisses against his cheek. His cock jerked against Christian's buttocks. "Guess what? I want that, too."

He got his fingers to work, unbuckling Christian's belt and unfastening his trousers. He shoved Christian's chinos to mid-thigh. Christian's cock strained against his underpants. Slowly, Harry drew the tips of his fingers over the bulge, brushing the underside, before focusing on the ultra-sensitive tip with the lightest, most sensual touch.

"Oh, God." Christian shuddered. His dick was leaking…a lot. He could feel, without looking down, how damp the front of his underpants was.

"Feels like a big dick," Harry whispered right into his ear.

Christian guessed they were well matched, both around eight thick inches and uncut. "See for yourself," he said.

Harry let out a light chuckle before sliding his thumbs into the waist of his underpants and shoving them down with his chinos. Christian's cock sprang back, hitting his abdomen. Harry curled a determined hand around the shaft and cupped his smooth balls with the other. He gave both a gentle squeeze.

"Oh yeah. That feels perfect."

Christian pushed his arse against Harry's hips, enjoying the sensation of his bare skin against Harry's jeans. Harry released his cock and moved his hands back to his butt. He jiggled both cheeks, feeling their muscular weight.

"Put your hands against the wall," Harry instructed.

Christian did as he asked and widened his feet as far as his half-dropped pants would allow. Harry fell to his knees behind him, and when his hot breath swept across his buttocks, Christian's skin rippled with gooseflesh. Harry planted a soft kiss on one cheek then the other.

"I could tell, even through your clothes that you had a great arse," Harry murmured. "But, man, this is even more spectacular that I imagined."

Despite their flirting and the close bond they had developed in the last few days, Christian was surprised to learn that Harry had been looking at him that way. *Such a good-looking, sexy younger man.* Part of him struggled to understand why anyone in their twenties would be interested in a man his age. Harry was on his knees, kissing his arse. There was nothing to struggle with there. He had to get over these insecurities and enjoy every delicious moment.

Harry spread his cheeks and drew his tongue along the deep crevice.

"Oh, wow," Christian gasped, pressing his hot face against the wall. He grabbed the tails of his shirt and hitched them around his midriff to give Harry clear access. He dipped his knees and pushed back against his face. Harry seemingly had no qualms or reservations about eating his arse, murmuring with delight as he worked his tongue around the delicate contours of his opening, driving him crazy with the intensity of it all. Even the soft rasp of his beard against the sides of Christian's hairless crack was a delight.

"You shave your butt?" Harry asked when he sat back, sounding breathless.

"I shave everything," Christian replied, "except my head."

"Hot. Take off your clothes and let me see you."

Christian hauled his shirt over his head and flung it on the floor. He kicked off his shoes and struggled out of his chinos, pants and socks, before turning to face Harry, who remained on the floor, gazing up at him with a playful smile on his lips and hungry desire in his eyes.

Although he was self-conscious of their age difference, Christian had few hang-ups about his body. He looked after himself. When he wasn't on holiday, like now, he ate well, drank alcohol in moderation and went running three evenings a week. He had a lean, athletic figure with a muscular chest and flat stomach — no six-pack. He'd never had the time or the inclination to pursue such an unhealthy ascetic, but he was happy about the way he looked.

Judging from the wide smile on Harry's face, he was, too.

"Beautiful," Harry said, staring straight at his perfectly smooth cock and balls.

He ran his hand over Christian's torso, making him shudder.

"What's this?" he asked.

"Huh?" Christian looked down as Harry gently traced his fingers across a long-faded scar on his abdomen. "Oh, that's nothing, a bike accident when I was a teenager. I've had those scars for so long, I don't even notice them anymore."

"You poor thing." Harry leaned forward and pressed the softest kiss to the faint pink line.

Christian shuddered again.

Harry licked his lips. "Ready to fuck? I sure am."

Christian returned the grin. "I've been ready all day. Whatever you do, don't touch my cock too much. I'm so turned on it would be like pulling a trigger."

Harry got to his feet. "Right now, it's your arse I'm interested in."

"I'll be right back."

Christian rushed to the bathroom and retrieved a strip of condoms and a bottle of lube from his toiletry bag. When he returned, Harry had taken off his shoes and socks and was slipping his shirt from his shoulders. Christian took a sudden intake of breath. Harry had the strong arms and chest of a manual worker. His pecs and tight belly were coated with delicious dark-blond hair. There was some kind of Celtic tattoo design on his left shoulder. He flashed a shy-looking smile as Christian gazed at him.

"It's my turn to show what I've got," he said.

"It's all great so far," Christian said. His eyes followed the trail of hair down the centre of his abdomen, where it fanned wider beneath his navel, leading the way into his pants.

Harry stripped hurriedly. His cock was even thicker than Christian remembered. His foreskin had retracted, revealing the gloriously moist pink head.

Christian rushed over and wrapped his arms around him, going straight in for a deep, soul-kiss. They pressed their bodies together, hot, naked skin against skin. Harry moved his hands to Christian's arse again, gripping the flesh and pulling him hard against his hips. They ground their cocks together, both slippery with pre-cum. Christian moaned. This level of intense desire was something he hadn't experienced in years. *Have I ever wanted anyone as much as this?*

Harry took the condoms and lube from his hands and guided him to the bed. "How do you want this?" he asked softly.

"Any way I can," he replied. He climbed on the bed, shuffling to the top. With his head and shoulders supported on pillows, he spread his arms and legs, beckoning Harry to him. Harry grinned, maintaining eye contact as he crawled towards him. He knelt between Christian's legs and put on the condom.

"I'll be careful," Harry said as he squeezed lube into his palm and spread it over his cock from head to base. Then he put his fingers between Christian's buttocks and sought his opening, spreading lube around the rim before slowly entering and preparing the way. His touch was smooth and gentle. "This okay?"

Christian nodded. "I'm ready."

Harry hooked his elbows beneath Christian's thighs, raising his hips. Christian groaned from deep within his chest when the head of Harry's cock pressed against his hole. He caught his breath, and looking into Harry's eyes, he nodded.

There was no pain. After so long without sex, he'd expected there would be. His body unfurled, welcoming the hardness of Harry's dick, taking the girth. They moaned together. Harry leaned over him as he drove to the hilt, bending his head for a kiss, pushing his tongue into Christian's mouth. Christian put his hands on Harry's torso, marvelling at the strength and beauty of the man inside him.

"Is this okay?" Harry asked, breathing heavily into him.

"Mm-m. Fantastic."

Harry twitched his cock. Christian groaned with delight, and they both laughed.

"Feel good?"

"The best."

Bearing his weight on his hands and knees, Harry took up a slow thrust, sliding back and forth with a fluid motion. Christian leaned his head forward, searching for more kisses, wanting to consume as much of Harry as he could. The pleasure was insane. He couldn't remember anyone ever filling him so perfectly.

Soon they were soaked with sweat. Their skin was slick as they pushed against each other.

Christian was aware of Harry making most of the effort. After a while, he urged him to roll onto his back. Christian climbed on top and impaled himself once again, riding him to an exquisitely paced rhythm. There was no rush. He didn't want this to end. Harry put his hands on Christian's waist and gazed at his body through half-lidded eyes as he rose and fell on top of him. Harry's face flushed a deep shade of pink, and his blond hair was soaked with sweat. Christian pushed his fingers into the lush curls on his chest, steading himself on his large pecs.

When they moved again, it was onto their sides. Harry took him in a spoon position, wrapping his arms around him and entering from behind. The intimacy, the depth of penetration, was the most sensational yet, allowing Christian to push his arse against Harry's hips. Harry's breath quickened and a desperate sound entered his moans of pleasure. He moved his hand to Christian's cock then squeezed and jerked.

"I'm gonna come," he gasped. "Let me bring you with me."

Christian surrendered to him completely. Harry's thrusts became deeper and more purposeful as he neared the end. He moved his hand across Christian's cock, stroking him to the inevitable. Their cries became louder and more desperate, the tension in their bodies reaching a peak of intense torture — then it burst.

Harry thrust hard as he came, forcing his cock against Christian's prostate, taking him over the edge with him. Christian spurted all over the bed. He seemed to be endlessly coming, blowing off shot after shot of thick white cream.

"Oh, God," he gasped when the trembling ceased. He rolled against Harry's chest, feeling his heart hammer against his back. Harry put his hand on Christian's hip, holding him in place, their bodies locked together. His breath rasped against the back of Christian's head.

"Fuck," Harry said on a long exhalation.

"Totally," Christian gasped. "Are you okay?"

"Are you kidding? I've never been better."

They snuggled even closer. Harry kissed the back of Christian's neck. Christian savoured the fullness inside him. Harry didn't feel like he had softened in the slightest after coming. *The miracle of youth.* Christian remembered what it had been like when he was under thirty, too. He rebuked himself for the thought. Harry hadn't made a single remark about the difference in their ages. If it didn't bother him, Christian had to get over it, too.

"I'd better take this out," Harry said at last. "I think I probably overloaded this condom."

They both laughed. Christian held his legs apart while Harry carefully withdrew. He rolled onto his back, watching as Harry trod a heavy step to the bathroom. His meaty arse jiggled magnificently as he did. He returned with a towel, and they cleaned the wet stains Christian had left on the bed covers as best they could.

"Looks like I'm not the only one who blew a huge load," Harry said as he lay back down.

Christian rolled against him, pressing his naked body to his, draping an arm across his chest.

Incredible, he thought. He had come to Nyemouth hoping to find a story. He hadn't expected to find such intimacy and passion with a local boy.

Chapter Twelve

"What have you got to look so happy about?" Antoni asked as he approached Harry in the marina the next day.

"Aren't I allowed to smile?" he shot back with a breezy grin.

"Oh, that's more than a smile," Antoni said. "Besides, there aren't many people around here with much to be cheerful about lately." Antoni was dressed in jeans with a thick hoodie and a baseball cap. Though it was another sunny day, there was an autumn chill in the air that had not been there the day before.

"Where are you off to?" Harry said, changing the subject. He gestured to the camera hanging from a strap around Antoni's neck. He rarely went anywhere without it. "Taking photos today?"

"Maybe. The light is good. I thought I'd walk along the north pier, maybe the beach, and see if I can come up with something interesting. How about you? No charter today?"

"Tomorrow," Harry explained. "Fishing trip. The boat is already prepared, so I'm free until later. I'm having tea with my parents. If you're heading along to the pier, do you mind if I tag along? I might grab a bite and a coffee from one of the kiosks."

"I'd love that." Antoni checked his watch. "I could do with something myself. I hadn't realised it's almost lunchtime."

The sun was in their eyes as they walked along the harbour side. Harry had tucked his sunglasses into the neck of his shirt earlier. He pulled them out and slipped them on. The good weather had brought some late season day-trippers to the town, though he suspected the sensation caused by the double murder earlier in the week also had something to do with it.

"How are the Jasinski family doing?" he asked.

"Still in shock. I don't think it's sunk in yet. They are still so busy. The police are asking so many questions and going through Niko's personal things. And there are a load of people getting in touch and offering help, but really, they are just being nosy. I doubt they've had a minute to themselves all week. I've kept a distance myself, yesterday and today, but they know where I am if they want my help."

"You're a good friend, Antoni. I'm sure they appreciate it. They'll need people like you once it all this quietens down and those nosy bastards disappear."

"I'll be there, though I'm not sure they will ever come to terms with losing Niko. How could anyone?"

"How is Roger doing?" he asked about Antoni's brother.

"He's fine...as always. He's started seeing a girl from Morpeth, so he's in the early stages of love." Antoni laughed and rolled his eyes. "He wants to leave early tonight so they can go to the cinema. That's why I'm looking to take photos now. I need to get back to close the shop and gallery later."

They reached a line of kiosks at the end of the harbour. In days gone by, it used to be the old fish market. Now it accommodated a bunch of stalls selling seafood, baked goods, hotdogs and burgers...all the usual tourist fayre. Aware that he would be eating with his parents later, Harry wanted something light for his lunch and opted for a tray of fresh oysters from the fish seller.

"What about you?" he asked Antoni. "My treat."

"Oysters." He grimaced. "No, thank you. I'll have a tub of crayfish tails."

With a smile, Harry placed the order, keeping a keen eye on the man behind the counter to ensure his oysters were freshly shucked, which they were.

"Anything with them?" the man asked. "Onion? Tabasco sauce?"

"Just a wedge of lemon," he said.

Antoni wanted vinegar on his crayfish.

"Watch out for the seagulls," the vendor quipped as he handed them over.

Once served, they moved to the side of the quay. All the benches were taken with tourists, so they leaned against the low wall while they ate. Harry squeezed lemon juice over the three oysters on his tray and tipped the first one into his mouth, savouring the delicious salty flavour before swallowing.

"They look disgusting," Antoni said, eyeing his lunch with disdain.

"But they taste great."

He screwed up his face. "So you say. I have no intention of finding out." He mixed the crayfish with the vinegar in his tub before taking the first forkful.

A steady progression of people walked by as they ate. There were more tourists around than Harry had first thought. As it was school-term time, they were mainly older folk, retired types who had the luxury of taking a trip to the coast mid-week, the kind who usually came to Nyemouth for their fish-and-chip lunches and a walk along the beach. They would disappear mid-afternoon, ensuring they were home in good time for tea.

Antoni startled him by suddenly calling out in a loud voice, "Gemma."

Harry paused with a shell halfway to his mouth to follow his line of sight.

A young woman with long brown hair, fastened in a ponytail, turned at the sound of her name. Antoni raised his hand and beckoned her over. Her expression was miserable and barely improved as she came towards them. Harry recognised her as a part-time waitress at the Seagull Café. She was usually so cheerful and friendly with the customers. The change in her mood today was startling.

"Hey," Antoni said, "how are you?"

"I'm okay," she answered. Her face told a different story.

Her eyes were tracked with thin red lines. The skin below was puffy and dark. It was obvious she had been crying...and recently.

"You're not going to work, are you?" Antoni asked.

She nodded. "I'm going to be late."

"Can't you get some time off?"

She looked impatient. "I'd rather not. I want to work and keep busy. It stops me from thinking too much."

"Okay. Well, look after yourself."

"I will," she said, already walking away. "I have to go. It was nice to see you." She disappeared into the crowd.

Harry gave Antoni a quizzical look. "What was that about?"

"Gemma Payne. Niko's ex-girlfriend."

"Ah…right." Now her cried-out look made sense. "She seems to have taken it hard. How long had they been separated?"

"Not long. They split some time over the summer. Niko wouldn't tell his parents the reason why, but we heard rumours that Gemma dumped him when he cheated on her."

"Oh, shit. The poor girl. I guess she still has strong feelings for him."

Antoni nodded, taking another forkful of crayfish. He chewed, swallowed, then said, "I think she wanted to get engaged. That's what Niko told his parents, anyway. They thought he was too young, so I don't think they were greatly upset when they stopped seeing each other. Still, it must be painful for her now. Your feelings for a person don't stop just because you have split."

Harry sensed a barb in Antoni's last comment and didn't respond. He had been the one to call 'time' on their own relationship. Antoni had made no secret that was not what he wanted and had tried more than once to get back with Harry. Though things between them were amicable, Harry suspected Antoni wouldn't take much persuading to start again now. As far as he was aware, there had been no one else in Antoni's life since they'd broken up.

"Niko was twenty? Right?" he asked, swerving around Antoni's remark.

"Yes. Gemma is the same age, more or less. There may be a month or two on either side of their birthdays."

"So, who was this other person? The one he left her for?"

Antoni gazed at the passing crowd. "I have no idea. A young man like that will always keep secrets from his family and friends. I doubt it matters. It was probably nothing — a one-night stand or such like. He was likely just doing what everyone his age should do and just enjoying himself."

* * * *

Like most working men's clubs, the Nyemouth club looked like it hadn't been updated since the seventies or eighties. The wallpaper was a dull shade of yellowish brown, showing the stains from decades of tobacco smoke. The heavily patterned carpets were dirty and threadbare. The only sigh of modernisation was the fifty-inch TV mounted on the wall in the far corner. It was playing horse racing, which Christian suspected had been shown in here every day for forty years.

It was filled with the typical daytime drinking crowd — old men who nursed their pints and made them last, the drunks who could be found in any town, propping up whatever bar served the cheapest drinks. A bored-looking bartender in his late sixties looked put out every time a customer disturbed him from his newspaper for another drink.

What a depressing place.

Christian's investigation had brought him here as a last resort. He'd spent the day trying to find out as much as he could about the murders of Niko Jasinski and Ike Meeker. Though there was plenty of gossip to be heard throughout Nyemouth, there did not appear to be much substance to any of it. Idle speculation was all it had turned out to be.

He'd spent the morning in his hotel room searching the internet. Dominic had said something the other night that had stuck with him — that Niko had made money on the side with an OnlyFans account. As he'd tried to look further into the matter, he'd soon realised what a useless task it was. OnlyFans alone had well over a million content creators, and there were so many other sites offering a similar kind of service. The chance of locating Niko's profile in a sea of false identities and alter-egos was nil.

He wondered how relevant the fact was, if it was even true, to the case. So what if Niko was an online sex worker? It was hardly a big deal these days. One of Christian's friends in Manchester, Mark, an intensive care nurse, had been supplementing his income by selling daddy-themed sex videos for years. Mark made no secret of what he did, and most of his friends knew about it.

Though sex would always add spice to a murder investigation, Christian doubted it had anything to do with Niko or Ike's deaths, and quickly abandoned the search. He tried contacting Marie Baxter-Booth, the TV reporter he'd met on Tuesday, with no success. He left a message but had no hope she would call him back. She was likely off in another part of the county, covering another story. The news station would have no further interest in Nyemouth until there was an arrest or another murder.

He'd gone from the hotel to the Seagull Café for a coffee and a late breakfast. He'd been starving by then.

Harry had spent the entire night with him. When Harry had left that morning, the temptation to ask him to stay had been massive. Christian could easily have cancelled all his plans for the day and spent them in bed, fucking and ordering room service, but something made him hold back.

Things had moved so fast for the two of them, and it would do them good to spend a little time apart. They'd made a date for tomorrow night, once Harry returned from his fishing charter. That would have to do for now. Christian would only be here for another week. Who knew what would happen after that? It was best that they had some time apart from each other to process everything that had occurred.

For the rest of the day, he was determined to focus on work.

In the café, he'd eavesdropped on a couple of conversations before speaking to a middle-aged couple who seemed to know the Jasinski family. Keeping it casual, he'd drawn information out of them. Niko had had a full-time job at a food processing factory on an estate outside of town, but since he'd turned eighteen, he'd been earning extra cash as a bartender at the workingmen's club. Christian remembered Dominic and Jacob had also mentioned something about that. If the OnlyFans rumours were true, when had he found time to make his videos?

Christian drained the pint of lager he'd been drinking and approached the bar for another. The bartender put down his paper and enquired, "Same again?"

"Please," Christian said.

"Are you staying nearby?" the bartender asked, selecting a fresh glass from an upper shelf. His tone was friendly, sounding like he was genuinely interested.

"Is it that obvious I'm a tourist?"

The man chuckled. "Pretty much. Even though you've arrived at the arse end of the season. What made you choose Nyemouth?"

"I'm a friend of Dominic Melton. He recommended the place."

"And you listened to him?" the man laughed. "It's not my idea of a holiday destination. You should have gone to Benidorm or the Canary Islands at this time of year. I know I would."

"I'm not too keen on the hot temperatures there. This climate suits me fine."

The man looked unconvinced. "If you say so. In another month, it'll be Baltic around here. The winter sun becomes very tempting around that time." He set the drink on the counter in front of him. As Christian handed him a five-pound note, he saw the man examine him more closely. "You're not the fella who was on the boat with Harry Renner the other night, are you? When they found young Niko."

"I am," Christian said carefully. "I was the one who spotted him."

The man groaned. "What an awful business." He handed the note back to Christian. "Keep your money, son. This is on the house after all you've been through."

Christian feigned ignorance. "You knew him?"

The man nodded sadly. "He worked here on and off. He started collecting the empties for me before I moved him behind the bar. He was a lovely lad — a real grafter, you know, not like some of the other work-shy bastards around here. Even when he got another job, he would still help me out on the weekends. I could always rely on Niko when I was in a tight spot."

"It sounds like he had a strong work ethic."

"He certainly did. And that's a rare thing in the young 'uns these days. Believe me, I know. I've hired and fired enough of the useless buggers."

Christian sipped the beer and pressed on. He had to be careful dealing with people like this. As soon as they realised that they were talking to a journalist, they could clam up. Not that he was officially acting in a journalistic capacity here. "Do you have any theories about who might have done this?"

The man frowned. "There are enough people about who don't think much of outsiders, even when the family has been here for years, like Niko's folks have. There are some in Nyemouth whose attitudes haven't moved on since the nineteen-fucking-fifties. Excuse my French, but I can't imagine any of them doing more than running their big mouths off. What happened to Niko was just too…nasty."

"Hey," said Christian, "I didn't get your name."

"Jacky. I've been the steward here for twenty-seven years."

"Christian. It's nice to meet you, and thanks for the drink."

"It's my pleasure."

Christian took another sip. "So Niko never had any trouble with anyone here in the club?"

Jacky shook his head. "No more than anyone. I won't put up with any of that racist crap. If I hear one wrong word from someone, they are barred. Of course, there are always the drunk idiots who don't know when they've had enough, but Niko had a good way with those people. He could usually get them off the premises before they caused any trouble. He was a lot more tactful about it than I ever am. I sling them out by force if I have to." He shook his head sadly. "Christ. He was a lovely kid. I'm going to miss him."

Christian knew when to quit. There was no point in pushing Jacky for further information. He didn't know any more about Niko's death than the other people he'd spoken to. Whatever he said would be speculation and nothing more. He thanked him again for the drink and returned to his seat.

Niko Jasinski was an enigma. Apart from the town racists who hated his Polish heritage, no one had a bad word to say about the boy. He was popular and respected, and yet someone had driven a knife into him and thrown him into the stormy sea. Christian would have to dig deeper if he was going to make headway on his story.

There must be more to Niko that these people were letting on.

He needed to find out what.

Chapter Thirteen

Harry's Friday fishing charter consisted of three lawyers who wanted to celebrate the forthcoming retirement of one of their group. They were all in their late sixties, and it had not been obvious at first which one of them was retiring. The lucky man was called Clive and was actually in his early seventies.

"There's a big lunch planned for next week with speeches and all that malarky," Clive had explained. "But I wanted to do something a bit more relaxing than that."

All three of the men were senior partners in a law firm in Newcastle and agreed they wanted to do something for themselves before their younger colleagues took over and forced them into something more social. Harry had laughed and given them exactly what they wanted. The men had brought their own equipment. All he had to do was provide them with the boat, bait and refreshments.

It was another unseasonably mild day. The swell was deeper than when he'd come out with Christian on

Wednesday, but it was perfect fishing weather. He took *The North Star* two miles north of Nyemouth and a mile and half offshore, letting it drift in the current while the men fished off the stern. Most fishing charterers started on the beer before they had even left the harbour, but by mid-morning the strongest drink these old boys had taken was coffee.

Reece Wallace, Harry's temporary boat hand for the day, came up the ladder from the lower deck with a fresh cafetiere in one hand and a carton of milk in the other.

"Want a refill before I top these guys up?" Reece asked.

"Sure. Thanks." Harry held out his empty mug.

Reece filled it three quarters full before splashing in the milk.

Harry had been relieved to enlist Reece's help at such short notice. It had been late on Thursday afternoon when Tom had texted to say he was ill and couldn't make it. When Harry had called him back, his phone had gone straight to voice mail. It was out of character for Tom to miss work like that, especially for the second time in a week. Harry deduced there were two likely reasons and wanted to speak to his cousin first-hand to determine which it was. It was possible Tom was genuinely sick, in which case he wanted to know if there was anything he could do to help. Tom's son had been off school earlier in the week, so he could have caught something from him.

It was also very unlikely. Tom had a steely work ethic and rarely allowed illness to keep him down. Cold, flu, headaches, upset stomachs? They didn't faze him. Tom would swallow whatever medication he needed and get on with the job. He'd always been very vocal in the past about people who shirked their responsibilities and took sickies for hangovers or minor runny noses.

The second option was far more troubling to Harry. Was Tom experiencing some kind of PTSD in the wake of Niko's death? He'd come down to the harbour to help Harry clean the boat out Tuesday but hadn't been back since. Was he afraid to return? Had what he'd witnessed and been a part of on Monday affected him more deeply than he'd let on? There would be no easy answer or solution to a problem like that, but if that was the reason for his absence, Harry would do everything he could to help his cousin though it.

Harry had gotten so used to dealing with traumatic events as part of his lifeboat service that he'd forgotten how distressing they could be for regular people.

Harry had always had a strong and open relationship with his parents. He'd been able to tell them anything since he'd been a boy. Tom had not had the same privilege. His parents were the type who used to laugh at his emotions and tell him to toughen up. Maybe he was repressing his feelings about the murder.

Of course, Harry knew he could also be worrying over nothing, and Tom might have a dodgy gut that he didn't want to talk about. The sooner Harry spoke to him, the happier he would feel. If he hadn't answered his phone by the time they got back to shore this afternoon, he would go around to his house.

Reece returned to the wheelhouse with the empty cafetiere. "They say they'll have lunch around one. I'll go down and get it ready in a few minutes."

"Thanks, Reece. I really appreciate you doing this."

The boy grinned. "I had nothing else on today. Besides, this is going to be great for my socials." He took out his phone for what seemed like the hundredth time that morning and took a selfie. "Come on. Get in the shot."

"No thanks." Harry waved him away. "Take all the pictures you want, but leave me out of it."

Like most of the people Harry knew his age, Reece seemed to be obsessed with social media. It was a fad he had never gotten into or even understood that much. He was in a WhatsApp group with some of the lifeboat crew and had a Facebook profile he rarely used. He only ever looked at that to see what his distant relatives who didn't live in Nyemouth, were up to. Harry hated having his photo taken and couldn't fathom why so many people like Reece wanted to post their selfies online for a stranger to judge and pull apart.

"Suit yourself," Reece said, backing onto the open deck with his phone raised high for another picture. He did the held tilt and sucked-in cheeks pose that seemed to be the way for all selfies. "You should set up an account...or a YouTube page. You'd get so many followers. 'The Lonely Seaman.' That's what you can call yourself and post loads of moody pics and clips of you out on the boat. My God, the girls would go insane for that."

Harry laughed. "Give over, will you? I'm not doing any of that stuff."

Despite his obvious vanity, Reece was a fun, easy-going boy—nothing like his miserable dad. Stew had been moping around the harbour with a face like a smacked arse when he'd overheard Harry telling another fisherman about Tom being sick. It was Stew who had begrudgingly suggested his son take his place.

"It'll do the little bastard good to put in an honest day's work," Stew had grumbled.

Harry had known the boy since he was young. The work was essential but undemanding, and he'd been delighted when Reece had agreed to come along today.

"So, is this where it happened?" Reece asked, standing in the middle of the deck. "With Niko?"

Harry silenced him with a gesture and jerked his head into the boathouse. "Quiet," he whispered, once they were both inside. "I don't think those guys know, and I'd like to keep it that way."

Reece's cheeks flushed pink. "Sorry. I didn't think."

"It's all right. Just don't go scaring my customers off, okay? I need those guys to go home and tell their rich old friends what a great time they had and how much fun my fishing charters are."

Reece glanced at the three lawyers. "I don't think you need to worry. They're having a grand old time."

"Let's keep it that way, eh?"

"You know, if you had a great social media profile, you wouldn't have to worry about that. People would be queuing up to come on one of your trips. Post a few pictures with your top off. 'Sexy fisherman', that kind of thing, and you'll be the hottest new thing."

Harry laughed. Reece was possibly the most endearingly naïve guy he'd ever met. His ideas were ridiculous, but it was impossible not to like him. "The only hot thing I'm interested in now is lunch. Get downstairs and make a start so we can feed my customers on time."

* * * *

"Would you like to sit here?" Christian gestured to an empty table outside the coffee shop. "It's a nice afternoon. We should enjoy it while we can."

Gemma Payne shook her head. "No. Let's go in. I don't want anyone seeing me talking to you. I'll only get more grief for it."

She marched inside. Christian followed in her wake until she chose a seat in the rear corner, as far from the door and windows as she could get.

"What would you like?" he asked, keeping his tone light and friendly. "They have some delicious looking cakes on the counter."

Gemma glanced at her watch. "A small cappuccino," she said curtly. "Nothing else."

"I'll be right back."

They were on the old side of the town, down one of the back streets. He'd spotted this place while wandering the other day, but this was his first time inside. Gemma Payne was on a break from her job at the Seagull Café and had insisted they meet somewhere out of the way. A combination of nosiness and good luck had brought him into contact with Niko Jasinski's ex-girlfriend. He'd spent a couple of hours in the working men's club yesterday afternoon, plying the daytime drinkers with free booze as they told him everything they knew about Niko. Most of it was third-hand gossip and guesswork, but he'd struck gold with the information about his ex.

Christian placed the order and returned to the corner, where Gemma gazed blankly at the screen of her phone. She put it face down on the table when he sat.

"Nice place," he said.

She screwed her face. "It's purely for the tourists. Overpriced and all style over substance. The Seagull is miles better."

"Have you been working there long?"

"About a year. Just part-time while I'm at college."

"Oh, really. What are you studying?"

She glowered at him. "I thought you wanted to talk about Niko, not me."

She wasn't going to make this easy for him.

"I'm sorry," he said, keeping it friendly despite her tone. "Habit, that's all."

Her eyes bore into his. Christian had no idea why she'd agreed to speak to him, but now that she was here, he had to make the most of it and not piss her off. He smiled softly, and she looked at her hands on top of the table.

"How long were the two of you dating?"

"Probably a year...maybe a little longer." She gnawed at a fingernail. "Yeah. We met around spring last year. We were seeing each other by Easter."

"And how was he? As a boyfriend, I mean."

Gemma sighed. "You know, all anyone is saying about him now is how wonderful he was. Such a great guy. Mister Perfect. I bet that's what everyone else you've talked to has said. Right? I suppose that's what people do when somebody dies, isn't it? They only remember the good stuff."

"Don't you?"

A grimace. "No one is perfect, despite what they're saying now. He hurt me like no one else ever has. He was a bastard when he wanted to be."

Gemma clammed up when the waiter arrived with the drinks. They sat in silence as the coffee cups were laid out. Christian smiled politely until they were alone again.

"Go on."

"The whole time we were together, there was only him. I didn't even look at other guys. I get plenty of attention, you know. I don't always look like this. When I go out, when I'm dressed up, I can turn a few heads. But I didn't give any of the men who chased me a second look. I was Niko's girlfriend, and that meant something—at least it did to me."

Gemma was clearly in a lot of pain. Whatever hurt Niko had inflicted on her had not been resolved, and now his untimely death had added grief and anger to her burden.

"He cheated on you?"

There were no tears in her eyes. She was too cross for that. "Big time. While I was saving myself for him, he was giving it to any slag who looked at him. You should have seen some of the videos on his phone. It was...porn. That's how I found out. He left his phone on the sofa while he went to collect a pizza. I'd heard rumours, but I didn't believe them, so I had a look for myself."

Christian had heard it all before. If someone was prepared to go snooping, they had to be prepared for what they found.

"What pissed me off the most was the way he brushed it off," Gemma continued. "When I confronted him with what I'd found, he said it wasn't what it looked like, that I didn't understand. There was video evidence of him fucking other girls. What was there to understand?"

"Maybe the clips were old. Could they have been of former girlfriends?"

"I checked the date stamp. They were not old. Besides, Niko got a new tattoo while he was with me. I recognised it in more than one of the videos."

Christian's mind was already turning. If Niko had been a player, sleeping with lots of other girls, maybe his death was a crime of passion. He could have been attacked by a jealous boyfriend—or a woman who thought he'd taken advantage of her. Everyone had secrets. Sometimes those closest to a person didn't know them as well as they thought.

Gemma was right. All he'd heard about Niko until now was what a great guy he had been. No one was ever perfect. Niko was as flawed as any other human.

"What about his murder?" he asked. "Do you know anyone who'd want to hurt him?"

Gemma looked him straight in the eyes. "Apart from me, you mean?"

"That's not what I said. Did you recognise any of the girls on his phone? Could one of them have held a grudge against him? Or maybe they had boyfriends."

"Fuck knows," she said through gritted teeth. "I didn't recognise them, no. They all had that cheap wannabe porn-star look. You know, massive hair, big tits, shaved minge. I thought he had better taste than that. Obviously not."

"What about—?"

"No." Gemma got to her feet. "This was a mistake. I thought talking would make me feel better. It hasn't. It just…makes me sick."

She covered her face to hide the tears as she rushed out of the coffee shop.

Chapter Fourteen

Christian remained where he was to finish his coffee after Gemma's abrupt exit. That the girl was upset was evident. There was no point in rushing after her with more questions. He wasn't investigating Niko Jasinski's murder. The police were. He was here seeking inspiration for a novel, and he had certainly found it. Niko had been a complex young man, and Christian's brain was already putting the pieces together to form a fascinating character.

He opened his notebook and jotted down his thoughts. It would be crass, not to mention heartless, to write a barely fictionalised account of the boy's murder, but he could take elements of his life to form the spine of his story. Using Nyemouth as a backdrop, he would write about the troubles and danger experienced by a young guy in the town.

His main character could be an amalgam of all the men he knew here — Niko, Dominic, Arnie, even Harry. There were facets to all of them that intrigued him. He still didn't know what the plot of the book would be, but that didn't worry him. It would come later. Character was the most important element of any novel.

After half an hour, he was done. He checked the time...almost five. He had a date with Harry at seven. Christian gathered his stuff and shoved it into his brown leather satchel. He should head back to the hotel. He wanted to shower and change before they got together.

A deliciously warm sensation spread through his chest at the thought of Harry. They hadn't seen each other at all the day before, and the absence made his anticipation for tonight even stronger.

The ceiling of the coffee shop was low, with thick wooden beams creating a gloomy atmosphere. It was a relief to step outside into daylight. It would be dark in an hour or so, but for now, the sky remained clear and blue. It was a beautiful indication of the evening ahead.

He was at the top of South Bank, the long, cobbled street that ran parallel to the harbour. Christian slung his bag over his shoulder and started the downward trek to the bridge and his hotel. He was lost in his head, and it took a moment to acknowledge some kind of commotion taking place ahead of him.

There were four people outside the Nyemouth and Northumberland Gallery, a small studio he'd been meaning to visit, which specialised in original artwork and photographs of the local area. Two men in their thirties stood in the doorway of the gallery, while outside a man and woman faced up to them.

"Fuck off back where you came from," the man shouted. He was thickset with a heavy, potato-like head. His face was screwed into an ugly expression. His hair was shaved to a dark stubble, which only made him more unattractive.

"Polish cunts," barked the woman. With greasy black hair scraped into a ponytail, she was as physically unpleasant as her companion. Unlike the man, her face shone with delight. She was enjoying the wretched spectacle they had created.

The two men in the gallery showed extraordinary restraint.

"Just leave before we call the police. You've been warned before. This is harassment," one of the men said.

They were very similar in appearance — tall, athletically built, good-looking, with light-brown hair and high cheekbones. They both wore chinos and plain blue shirts. There was maybe a year or two difference in their ages and Christian decided they had to be brothers.

"Call the fucking police," Potato-head sneered. "Like we give a shit. We just want rid of all the dirty Poles like you. You've ruined this fucking town."

"Dirty bastards," the woman jeered.

"Fucking stinking," the man continued.

"Homos as well," the woman said, cackling now.

"Aye. Polish queers. For fuck's sake, man. As if we haven't got enough queer fuckers of our own without having the take in Poland's bum-boys as well."

Christian had heard enough. The gallery owners might be too mild mannered to deal with these arseholes, but he wasn't. He stepped forward.

"You can add Norway to your list," he said, getting in the man's face. *Jesus. He's even uglier up close.*

"Huh?" The man took a step backwards, looking Christian over with tight, piggish eyes.

"Norway," he said calmly. "You can add Norwegian to your list of international queers. Me." He took a step forwards, getting back up in the man's face.

Potato-head looked at the woman for support.

"What the fuck is this?" she screeched.

Christian shot her a venomous look. "It looked a lot to me like harassment — racist and homophobic. Those two aggravating factors should go down well when you're up in front of the magistrates." He turned his head to the men in the gallery. "Go on and call the police. I'll be happy to make a witness statement so you can press charges against this pair of layabouts."

The man backed off again. His nasty expression had been replaced by that of a petulant child. Christian could almost see the cogs turning in his tiny brain. He didn't give him a chance to think before stepping forward again. He poked a finger into the centre of the man's chest. "What's wrong, little man? You seemed to have plenty to say before." He jabbed him again. "Eh?"

"Get your gay fucking hands off me," he said petulantly, turning away from him.

"Fuck off," Christian shouted. "The pair of you. *Now*."

The man jumped then turned around, hurrying down the street. The woman shot Christian a rancorous look before shuffling after him.

Christian turned back to the men at the gallery. "Are you guys okay?"

They both greeted him with a smile.

"Sure. Even better after that," one of them said.

"You didn't really have to do that," the second man said. "They make a lot of noise, but they aren't any serious risk. More a nuisance. But thank you anyway. That was the best laugh I've had all week."

Christian sighed. "I can't stand bullies of any kind. When I see shit like this, I have to call it out."

"That was Dean and Linda Bewick, our resident bigots. They are right pains in the arse, the pair of them. I don't think they are all there, like children."

Christian shook his head. "No, they knew what they were doing. There was no excuse for it."

The men introduced themselves as Antoni and Roger.

Antoni. Harry's ex. Of course. He'd said something the other night about his Polish ex and the regular racist abuse he suffered.

Christian gave him a closer look. He was handsome, very, with a serious face and dark-grey eyes. Harry had good taste.

"Christian Coster." He shook their hands. "I meant what I said…about the police. You should call them and report this. Give them my name and tell them I'm staying at Quay House. They can find me there for a statement. This kind of abuse has to go on record if they're ever going to establish the size of the problem."

* * * *

With Reece's help, Harry had the boat cleaned down and all the equipment packed up by five-thirty.

"Thanks for everything today," he said, handing the boy his payment in cash. "You've been a great help."

Reece's eyes shone as he took the money. "I've enjoyed it. I used to hate it when my dad dragged me out on his boat when I was a kid, but this has been fun."

"I guess entertaining some well-off old guys on a leisure trip is a lot different from the kind of professional fishing your dad does."

"And then some. But it's not just that. My dad is a total pain most of the time, especially when he nags me to join him in the fishing industry—like there's any future in that." He rolled his eyes. "At least you're cool. If you ever need help again, put me at the top of your list."

"I will do." It was nice to meet a young man with so much enthusiasm. "What are you up to tonight? Going out?"

"Yeah. A group of us are heading into Morpeth. I'd better get a move on. Our lift is picking us up at seven."

Harry thanked him again and Reece climbed up the ladder to the dock and disappeared. Harry smiled at the idea of being cool. *That's the last thing I am.* Especially after Reece's earlier comments about his non-existent social media profile. The boy had continued to pester him for the rest of the afternoon until Harry gave in and posed for a selfie with him, just to shut him up. Later in the day, Reece had stripped off his shirt and took even more photos of himself with the seascape behind him. That level of vanity had to be exhausting, Harry concluded.

At least Reece had done everything he'd asked of him without complaining.

Harry locked the cabin and climbed up to the dock. He had another charter tomorrow, just a half-day. If Tom was still sick, he could manage on his own. He checked the weather forecast on his phone. Saturday was on track to be good for most of the day, though it looked like it would all change by evening, with strong winds and rain moving in from the north-west. Sunday was set to be abysmal. Maybe he could spend a lazy day in bed with Christian.

The idea alone sent a rush of endorphins through him.

Time to get home and make himself presentable for their date tonight.

As he walked along the riverside, he tried Tom's number again. Surprisingly, he picked up on the third ring.

"Hey." Tom sounded cheerful.

"Hey. How are you feeling?"

"Much better. Sorry for standing you up at short notice. I just couldn't leave the house."

"What was wrong?"

"Gippy guts. I think I picked it up off Joshua. We had to keep him off school earlier this week."

Harry exhaled. It sounded like a genuine excuse. His earlier concerns about Tom and his mental health were unfounded. He should have known better. Tom wasn't the type to let things get him down. He'd have been upset if it had been one of his family members or close friends, but he'd barely known Niko Jasinski. "I'm glad you stayed away," he said playfully. "That little toilet on the boat couldn't have coped with you dropping your guts all day."

Tom laughed. "You're not kidding, cousin. How did it go today?"

Harry told him about Reece and the fishing party.

"Reece seems like a good lad," Tom said. "Nothing like his miserable dad. God, I swear he's getting worse. You should have heard him mouthing off around the harbour the other morning. He's a real prophet of doom these days. He needs to lighten up."

"Yeah, Reece must take after his mother. He's nothing like Stew." Harry reached the front of his house. He waited outside, continuing the call. "He said I need to have a social media presence. You know, for the boat."

"You do. I've thought that for ages."

"Why didn't you say something?"

"Cause I knew I'd be wasting my breath."

"I've already got a website."

"And you never update the fucker," Tom said. "There's no facility to book trips or buy tickets. It's very...basic."

"It takes too much effort to update the bloody thing. I don't understand how it works."

"That's why social media is a better option. It takes seconds to update."

"Hmm."

"Listen... I'll take some pictures when we're out tomorrow — the boat, the coast, you. Then I'll set up a profile for you over the weekend and show you how easy it is. It'll get much more attention than that dreary website of yours."

"Huh. Thanks for the encouragement," he said dryly.

"You'll thank me next week."

"I'd better go," Harry said. "I've got a date and need to change."

"Whoa, hold on. Not so fast. A date. Who with?"

Oh, what the hell. Might as well tell him.

"Christian," Harry said.

"Who's that? Oh, wait. The writer dude from Monday?"

"Yes," he said, experiencing a strange giddiness just talking about him.

"I didn't know you liked him."

"Neither did I," Harry admitted. "Not in the beginning. It just kind of happened."

"Good for you. Go for it. He seems like a nice bloke."

"He is." Harry found it difficult not to gush. "He's affected me in a way I didn't think possible. I know I need to be cautious. After what went down on Monday, my emotions are probably a little unstable at the minute, but I feel calm when I'm with him. And he's so easy to talk to. I feel like I've known him for far longer than these few days."

"Oh, fuck caution," Tom said. "What happened to Niko and that other guy should have taught you to appreciate how short life is. Anything could happen at any time. Don't put something off until tomorrow because you might not get a chance to do it. Go on that date tonight and do every fucking thing you can imagine with him."

There was an ache in Harry's cheeks from smiling so much. "I didn't expect to get relationship advice from you."

"Well, you'd better take it, cousin. I'm older, wiser and married. I know what I'm talking about. Now, get off this damn phone and get your fishy arse in the shower. Christian doesn't want to smell that boat stink on you tonight."

Harry laughed out loud. "All right. I'm going. See you tomorrow."

"I'll be there, waiting for all the juicy details." Tom laughed again and hung up.

Tom had a blunt way of putting things, but Harry knew he was right. He wanted to appreciate every second of his time with Christian and hurried inside to get ready.

Chapter Fifteen

"I met your ex today," Christian said. "Antoni."

They lay in Harry's bed, basking in the afterglow of terrific sex. The plan had been for them to go out to dinner after he'd given Christian the tour of his home, but just like their date earlier in the week, passion had taken over, and when he showed him the bedroom, they didn't get any farther.

They lay on their backs, side by side, one leg entwined with the other beneath the covers. Outside, the harbour was filled with the noise of a busy Friday evening, but in here it was just the two of them, in a world of their own, intimate and close.

"How come?" Harry asked.

"I was passing by the gallery when I walked into a confrontation between Antoni and Roger with a couple of Nyemouth hoodlums, a bit like the situation you told me about the other day."

Harry rolled over, rising onto one elbow. "Aw, shit. Not again. Are they okay?"

Christian remained on this back, though his eyes moved sideways to look at him. "I think so. It was a verbal altercation—nothing violent and no damage was done. It was that awful brother and sister. What are their names again?"

"The Bewicks, Dean and Linda."

"That's them."

"Bastards. These fucking numpties have nothing better to do with their idle lives than cause trouble for decent people. I went to school with Dean. He was always a prick, and he hasn't changed."

"What's their problem? Apart from being brain-dead bigots."

"Oh, they're just typical small-town trash, the type you find everywhere. Their lives are a mess of drugs, booze and petty crime—in and out of jail on pathetically short sentences, never off probation, begrudging anyone else who might have achieved something with their own life. Antoni and Roger have had trouble with that pair since they opened the place, like art means a thing to those stupid pricks. They don't give a shit about the gallery. They just hate the guys because of their race."

"I talked them into reporting the incident to the police. I think they were just going to let it slide otherwise."

"Yeah. The police won't do much about an incident such as that. They aren't interested in preventing crime. They will only take action after an assault has been committed."

"Reporting it will help, though. If anything else happens, there will be a record."

Harry leaned in and kissed him on the cheek. "Mm-m. That's one of the things I'm coming to like about you. You're not as cynical as I am. I'd tie an anchor around the Bewicks' necks and dump them off North Point if I had my way. It would do the town and the taxpayer a big favour."

Christian shuffled around to look at him. His eyes were fiery pools in the lights from the bedside tables. "I'm rather enjoying it. You know, this small-town intrigue."

"I'm glad we amuse you." He gave him another kiss. "What did you think of Antoni?"

"We only spoke for a few minutes. He seems nice. They both do. Good-looking, friendly."

Harry trailed his fingers across Christian's smooth chest. "He is. He's really nice. We actually get on better now that we're not in a relationship than we did before. I think we were always intended to be friends. I hope he finds someone who appreciates him soon. He deserves that. He always wanted for us to move in together, but I couldn't go there. I'd like for him to meet someone who wants the same things that he does."

Christian put his hand on the side of Harry's face and drew him down for a kiss. They moved their lips softly over each other's. Ten minutes ago, they had been fucking hard and fast, now everything was calm.

"I think I'm done talking about your ex," Christian said, and they both laughed.

"You brought him up," Harry said, tweaking one of Christian's nipples.

"And I'm dropping him…for now. Should we think about going for some dinner soon?"

"Are you hungry?"

Christian nodded. "I've worked up an appetite."

"It's nearly nine. We'll struggle to find anywhere with a table at this time on a Friday."

"It doesn't have to be anything special. How about a takeaway?"

"There's a great fish and chips shop just along the street from here. We could collect something and bring it back."

"Sounds perfect."

Christian rolled over and swung his legs over the edge of the bed. Harry stayed where he was, taking a moment to watch his lover as he stood and searched for his clothes, which had been scattered around the room in their haste to get naked. His body was glorious. Tight and toned, with a few stretch marks and scars to prove his age.

"You never really told me the story behind those," Harry said.

"What's that?" Christian paused with one sock in his hand.

"The scars...on your arm and torso. Is it anything you can talk about?"

Christian looked down at himself. "You know, they are so old and faded that I don't even notice them." He brushed his fingers along the jagged line across his belly. "Nothing exciting. It was a motorbike accident when I was nineteen. My parents warned me not to get a bike, but I wouldn't listen. Cars were boring. I wanted the freedom, to go wherever I wanted or some such bullshit. I was going too fast on a wet and winding road. Thankfully, no one got hurt but me."

Harry bounded from the bed to him. He wrapped his arms around Christian and pulled him into a firm embrace.

"What's this?"

Harry pressed the full length of this bare torso against Christian's, relishing the contact of skin on skin.

He ground his hips, pressing their soft penises together. "I just wanted to enjoy your nakedness for a few seconds more before you put your clothes on." He rested his chin on Christian's shoulder and grabbed his arse in both hands.

Christian did not resist. "You're a strange young man, you know that?"

"Oh, absolutely. I always have been. I hope that's not a bad thing." He gave his butt a good squeeze.

"You don't hear me complaining, do you?"

* * * *

Harry set the table in his small kitchen-cum-dining room, putting out placements, cutlery and condiments. Christian had gone to the fish-and-chip shop to collect their dinner. As Harry pottered about from cupboard to table, barefoot in jeans and an old T-shirt, he realised how remarkably relaxed he was about this, so different from when he'd been with Antoni. He'd never felt entirely at ease when Antoni had come to his home, and he had preferred to spend time at Antoni's place instead, where he'd always have the option of leaving at the end of the evening.

Harry's home was very much his own, and it always felt like other people were intruding. He had twice brought back random hook ups and had hated every moment, rushing through the motions so they could hurry up and leave.

Though they hadn't made any definite plans for this evening, he'd expected they would go out for food and a few drinks before spending the night in Christian's hotel room. But when Christian had arrived for a quick look around his house, Harry hadn't wanted him to leave. Now here they were, ditching the Friday night lights of Nyemouth in favour of a takeaway and a quiet night in, and nothing made him happier.

Harry put on some music and took a bottle of beer from the fridge. He walked into the living room, which looked directly onto the harbour, and sipped from the bottle as he watched the reflections on the still water. At the beginning of the week, he would never have imagined himself in this situation, but so much had happened since then that he could barely get his head around it. The start of a relationship seemed rather minor next to everything else.

He saw Christian coming back along the waterfront and his heart gave an unexpected leap.

What the hell is going on with me?

Unable to control his eagerness, Harry hurried to the front door and was waiting when Christian arrived.

"Hey," Christian said, beaming as he came up the path. "You've got no shoes on. You'll catch your death of cold."

"Not with you to keep me warm." He winked. "Besides, we're made of strong stuff here on the northeast coast. It takes more than a chill to keep us down."

"I don't doubt it." Christian kissed him on the lips. "I know what you're capable of already. I felt it in my butt all the way to the shop and back."

"Oh. Are you okay? I didn't hurt you, did I?"

"Not a bit. It feels fantastic, actually."

"I've set the table," Harry said, leading him through to the kitchen. "I usually have food like this flopped out in front of the TV, but tonight I decided to make an effort."

"I'm okay eating off my knee. You don't have to go to any trouble just for me."

"It's no trouble. Besides, I wanted to." Harry got another cold beer and handed it to him. He looked Christian over, fascinated by the way his hair was swept back from his forehead and by the flecks of grey in his beard — a colour that matched his eyes.

Christian put the bag of food on the counter and clinked bottles with him. "Cheers."

"Cheers." Harry couldn't control the silly grin on his face. He took two plates out of the warm oven and started unwrapping the food.

"The chippy was busy," Christian remarked.

"It always is, especially on the weekend. At least you know they are cooking everything to order."

"I did a bit more eavesdropping while I waited. It's amazing some of the stuff you pick up."

Harry shot him a bemused look. Christian seemed to do a lot of that. "Oh, yeah. What did you hear?"

"Niko and Ike. It's still the only thing people are talking about. Understandably so. Everyone is still in shock and trying to make sense of what has happened. Most of it is crap, but something stuck out because it's not the first time I've heard it."

Harry emptied one portion of fish and chips onto a plate and unwrapped the second one. "What is it?"

"Have you ever heard anyone talk about Niko having an online sex account? You know, OnlyFans, JustFor.Fans, that kind of thing?"

"No. Did he?"

"I don't know. Dominic mentioned it the other night. It was a rumour he had heard, too. And some people were saying the same thing in the takeaway."

Harry served up the second portion. Christian had also bought a large tub of mushy peas. He spread it between their plates and used a tea towel to carry them to the table. "Like you said, gossip. I wouldn't take much notice of it. As if what happened to Niko wasn't bad enough, people want to trash his reputation now."

"So, you don't think it's true?"

Harry shook a good amount of salt and vinegar over his food. "I don't know. Doubt it really matters much. Loads of people sell videos on those sites now. It's not that unusual. He was a good-looking lad. I don't see the harm if he wanted to make money like that."

"I met his girlfriend today."

Harry's smile stiffened. "You did? How? Why?"

Christian had just put a chip in his mouth. He chewed and swallowed. "These are good. I met her as part of my investigation. I wanted to know more about Niko."

"I thought you intend to write this as fiction."

"I do, but I'm curious. It comes with the job. And I always do thorough research."

Harry softened and tucked into his meal. "Okay. What did she say?" He thought about when he'd seen her yesterday, when he'd been with Antoni — how tense and unhappy she had looked.

"She told me the reason they broke up was because he'd cheated on her. She found videos on his phone of him shagging other girls. But as I was walking back just now, it made me wonder. What if he wasn't cheating in the usual sense? What if the girls in his videos were other content creators, and they'd filmed themselves purely for business purposes? He might not have had any emotional connection with those girls at all. It might have been nothing but a business transaction."

"I don't think that would make Gemma feel any better. Whichever way you look at it, he still fucked other women behind her back...*allegedly*." Harry caught Christian giving him the side-eye. "What? Oh, hang on. Now you think Gemma killed him because she was jealous of these videos?"

Christian gave him an amused, lopsided grin, raising his eyebrows. "Just an idea."

"For one of your stories, maybe. I don't think Gemma is the murdering type. From what I've seen, she doesn't have it in her."

"Oh, you'd be surprised what people are capable of. Don't underestimate anyone when it comes to murder. Jealousy can bring out the worst in the mildest of personalities — the very worst."

"No." Harry gave him a playful nudge. "You're wrong about that. I'm sure of it. We've had some crazy things happen in this town, but I don't buy the idea of Gemma murdering her boyfriend."

"You know her then?"

"Yeah, but not well," he admitted. "I know her from the café. She's a nice girl. I can just about accept the fact she dumped Niko over what she found on his phone. I don't blame her for that. But the other stuff? No way. She's not a killer."

"Maybe," Christian said. "Maybe not. I'm just doing research and haven't drawn any conclusions. But everyone, including you, has told me this is a strange town with some unlikely goings on. I wouldn't rule anyone out yet."

Harry displayed a wide grin. "I see. Does that include me?"

Christian gave him a wicked grin. "Well, there are three people I know for certain who are in the clear — those of us who were on the boat...you, me and Tom. Apart from us, I'd say everyone else in this town is a suspect."

* * * *

Antoni Nowak clenched his fists and tried to quell the heavy feeling in his belly. He paced the quayside, drawing in deep breaths of sea air, hoping to ease the tightness in his chest. The temperature was dropping as the evening drew on, but he was oblivious to the cold.

What the hell is happening?

The lights were on in Harry's ground-floor flat, and though the blinds remained open, he couldn't see anyone inside. Antoni knew the layout of the place well enough, and the kitchen was at the rear of the house. He wouldn't see anything unless he went around the back and climbed over the six-foot wall to the yard.

Antoni had been on his way to Harry's when he'd spotted Christian leaving the fish-and-chip shop. He'd wanted to talk to Harry about what had gone down with the Bewicks that afternoon. Roger had gone out for the evening, and Antoni had felt the four walls closing in on him. He'd needed someone to talk to.

It had been a surprise to see their rescuer step out onto the pavement ahead of him. Antoni had been on the verge of calling out to him when something made him hold his tongue, some kind of sixth sense that proved to be accurate. He followed Christian around the harbour, and it was no surprise when he arrived at Harry's open door.

The kiss he'd witnessed on the doorstep had hit him like a truck.

Harry and Christian were seeing each other. There was no other explanation. The tenderness of their lips as they met made their feelings evidently clear.

Why hadn't Harry mentioned this to him yesterday?

Antoni hunched over and pressed his fist to his mouth. He wanted to heave, but there was nothing there — nothing physical. The hardening ball of pain was something he would not be able to throw up.

How did they even know each other? Christian had told them he was here on holiday, staying at Quay House. How was it possible for him to get together with Harry at that time?

Unless they knew each other before? Unless Harry is the reason Christian is here in the first place.

He wondered again why Harry would not have mentioned it.

Struggling to control his ragged breathing, Antoni turned away from the house and walked unsteadily back towards the town centre.

Chapter Sixteen

Christian watched as Harry swung his legs over the side of the bed and stood. He crossed the room with heavy feet to open the curtains. It was still dark. The only light in the room came from the lamp on the bedside table. Christian adjusted his pillow and admired the sight of Harry's strong shoulders, his powerful back and the high mounds of his butt, those delicious cheeks covered in a light blond fuzz.

"Hm-m," Harry said, leaning closer to the window.

"Something wrong?"

"Fog. This was not in the forecast. Bugger."

Christian slid from the bed and crossed the room. He approached Harry from behind and wrapped his arms around him, resting his chin on his shoulder while putting his hands on the furry plain of his lower abdomen. He pressed a soft kiss against the side of his neck before turning his gaze to the window.

A dense cloud of fog filled the harbour. Christian could just about see the orange glow of the streetlights through the grey haze, but the boats and the river beyond were concealed by the eerie blanket. Visibility seemed to be about five or six yards.

"Wow. That's thick."

Harry pushed back against him and ground his hips in a slow, comfortable motion. His buttocks were warm and plump against Christian's hips. "Yep," he sighed.

"Does this mean your charter is off?" Christian knew Harry's bookings were in short supply now that autumn was rushing in, but a guilty part of him hoped it would be called off and they could spend the day together.

"It's too early to say. Coastal fog like this is unpredictable. Sometimes it settles in for the whole day, other times it comes and goes in an hour. I'll have to go down to the boat and get it ready for my client's arrival. They'll likely have set off by now. It might clear up by eight. We can even hold on until nine or ten if it looks promising. I don't want to let them down. And more importantly, I don't want to refund their deposit. If I can get them out to sea today, I will."

"Bummer. There was I wishing we could go back to bed." He squeezed him tighter.

Harry turned his head for a kiss. "I'd love to, but I need the work."

"I know you do. I'm selfish, that's all. I want you to myself."

"Mm-m, that's nice to hear. But you know this is only a half-day trip. I'll be done by mid-afternoon. That should give you time to recharge your batteries."

"Oh, you think I need some rest time, do you?" Christian scuttled his fingers over his sides, tickling him all the way up to his armpits.

Harry howled and spun around. He crouched over, trying to ward him off. "I thought I might have worn you out." He could barely get his words out for laughing so hard.

Christian pressed his advantage, backing him against the wall. His hands went to Harry's hips, and he leaned against him, chest to chest. "I'm not the knackered old thing you think I am." They brushed their lips together.

"I never said you were old. I just want you well rested, with a hundred per cent energy for what I want to do to you later."

"Now that sounds like a promise."

"It is a promise."

They kissed long and deep.

As much as Christian wanted to take it further, he agreed that Harry's fee-paying customers were more important.

Harry went for a quick shower while Christian got dressed.

"Want me to make you breakfast?" he called into the bathroom.

"Thanks for the offer, but I'm going to collect takeaways from the Seagull. Tom is back this morning and will expect his bacon sandwiches, too."

"I'd forgotten what a first-rate service you provide."

"Well, my clients might not make it to sea today, but if I keep them happy, hopefully they'll move their booking to another weekend rather than ask for a refund."

The fog had not relented when they left the house just after seven. If anything, Christian thought, it might have gotten worse. And it was still dark. They crossed the road carefully, watching for headlights in the impenetrable greyness. There was a chill to it, which caught in Christian's chest when he inhaled. He could hear the flowing river and the squawk of gulls, but there was little he could see but the path in front of him.

"This is creepy," he said. "Like something from a horror film."

"Nah. It's nothing. Just weather. You'll get used to it."

"Are you sure you should be going out to sea in this?"

Harry took his hand in the fog. The touch was warm and reassuring in the cold atmosphere. "Don't worry. I have no intention of going anywhere, not unless this clears completely. As thick as it is now, it might all be gone in ten minutes. When you run a boat, you need to hope for the best and be prepared to go on short notice when things improve."

They had reached the low harbour wall. Christian could make out the ghostly forms of the boats moored below.

When they came upon *The North Star*, he saw there was already a light on in the wheelhouse.

"Tom? Is that you?" Harry called out.

A moment later, the dim outline of his cousin appeared in the doorway. Tom crossed the deck until he stood directly below them.

"Shitty morning, eh?" he said.

"Yeah. How are you feeling?" Harry asked.

"A hundred per cent better. Don't worry. I'm fine."

I was impossible to see in the dark and the fog, but Tom sounded cheerful, just like Christian remembered from their first meeting.

"I've checked a couple of different forecasts," Tom said. "This shouldn't last. I think we'll be clear by eight. Eight-thirty at the latest."

"I hope you're right," Harry said. "The forecast last night didn't even mention fog."

"It'll be fine." Christian realised Tom's gaze was fixed on him, a mischievous expression on his handsome face. "So," he continued, looking from one of them to the other, "you two, eh? Out and about early this morning."

Harry let out a long-suffering sigh. "You'll hear all the gossip later." He looked at Christian and winked. "For now, we need to get ready on the off-chance things clear up. You keep doing what you're doing, and I'll go and fetch the breakfasts. You want your usual? Or are your guts still sensitive?"

"I haven't had anything decent in days," Tom protested. "Get one bacon butty with fried mushrooms and one sausage butty with a fried egg. Red sauce on the bacon and brown on the sausage. And a large latte with a Kit Kat. Four fingers."

Harry laughed. "Righto. I'll be back in about twenty-minutes."

Christian and Harry continued their walk along the waterfront.

"He seems chirpy," Christian said.

"Doesn't he just. He'll be pulling my leg about the two of us for the rest of the day."

"Is it a problem? You and me?"

"Oh, God, no," Harry said, taking his hand again. "Don't ever think that. Tom is just a typical cousin. He always winds me up about things. But if I'm happy, then so is he."

"I'm happy, too." Christian raised Harry's hand to his lips and kissed it.

Through the fog, he saw the illuminated sign for Quay House. They stopped outside, turning to face each other.

"So, I'll see you this afternoon?" Christian asked.

Harry licked his lips and nodded. "If the fog doesn't clear by ten, it will be sooner than that, but otherwise, yes. I'll text you when I'm finished, and I'll catch up with you wherever you are."

"I don't intend to go far. I'll be somewhere around the town. Maybe we can have a late lunch."

"Deal."

They kissed on the lips and said goodbye.

* * * *

"It's not looking good, is it?" said Jake Wrangler when Christian had placed the bumper breakfast order.

"Tom seems hopeful that the fog will clear."

"Fingers crossed."

There were around twelve customers in the Seagull. Harry knew that in another half hour, the place would be packed. The smell of frying bacon, eggs and fresh coffee was delicious.

He suddenly realised he was starving. He had worked up quite an appetite during the night. Christian had been insatiable. They both had, dosing for an hour or two, before one of them would reach over and they would start again. He smiled at the memory. He had fucked Christian one last time before they'd risen this morning. Harry worried about hurting him. He'd always found getting fucked to be more uncomfortable than any real pleasure, but Christian couldn't get enough of it. They were definitely well matched beneath the covers.

"Someone's in a good mood," Jake remarked, breaking the hot memory.

"Aren't I always? You know I'm a morning man."

Jake raised his eyebrows. His expression was as roguish as Tom's had been earlier. "Yeah, right?"

"How are you doing, anyway?" he asked, changing the subject. "We haven't really had a chance to talk since Monday."

Jake shrugged. "You know what it's like. You try not to dwell on the rescues that don't work out and just hope and pray that the next one turns out better."

"You were amazing...really. You did such a good job—how calm you were and the way you tried to stop Niko's bleeding. I don't think I would have handled it as well."

"You were there, Harry, and you did. Other captains might have panicked, but you kept your head and did what you could for him, too." He placed two takeaway coffees on a tray and set about the next two drinks. "How has it been for you? Going back on the boat, I mean."

Harry leaned on the counter. "It was a little strange on the first morning, but I've tried not to give it much thought. When I'm on the boat, it's work, and I can shut my mind off from what happened. It sounds cold, right? Heartless, even, but that's just the way it's been."

Jake gazed over his shoulder while continuing with the drink's order. "It's not cold at all. If that's what it takes for you to get on with life, then it's fine. You know what I was like after the thing with Vince? I could have sold the yacht and moved on, but I didn't. I got back on board because I love that boat and wouldn't let a bad experience spoil that."

Harry nodded. Jake had been the subject of a lifeboat rescue himself last summer following a nasty incident with his ex-husband onboard his yacht, The Golden Lady. He was right. Harry couldn't let the tragedy ruin his livelihood. He loved *The North Star*. As awful as Niko's death had been, he couldn't let it destroy that love.

"You can always come to me," Jake said, "if you want someone to talk to or even just to rant. After a trauma like this, part of the healing process usually involves anger. And it doesn't always come straight away. You might find you're mighty pissed off in a month or two, rather than now. I'm probably the only person here who understands a bit of what you're going to feel, so I'm here if you need me."

Harry was overwhelmed with gratitude. Emotion balled in his throat. He swallowed and coughed. "Thank you. I appreciate it. And I will. Maybe not just yet, but sometime."

Jake smiled kindly. "The door is always open."

"How has it been in here?" Harry asked. Another obvious change of subject, but he didn't want to dwell on these emotions. "After what happened on Monday, I mean."

Jake added another two coffees to the tray. "Honestly? It's been like sitting through a really bad Agatha Christie adaptation. I've heard the most barmy theories you can imagine. It seems everyone in Nyemouth is an amateur detective all of a sudden, and they've worked out who the killer is or what motivated them—crimes of passion, organised gangs, drug debts, people smuggling, a Tinder killer, suicide. I've heard it all. I'm glad the Jasinski family hasn't been in to hear the kind of shit people are saying."

Harry grimaced. "Crikey. Stew Wallace has been spouting some crackpot theories around the harbour, too, but not as mad as those."

"Oh yeah, work in a café long enough, and you'll hear it all."

Harry left in good spirits, though it was a struggle to carry the four coffees and a bag full of food. The fog was as thick as ever. It was quarter to eight now, so he doubted it would clear in time for the scheduled departure. Hopefully, the food and drink would keep the punters happy, and they might get away before nine.

It was lighter now, the fog seemed less ominous after sunrise, and there was traffic on the road, cars and vans moving slowly through the dense cloud. The forecast had been for a bright day ahead of further storms tomorrow. Hopefully, now that the sun was up, the fog would disperse quickly.

Harry picked his way along the harbour. As he passed Quay House, his thoughts returned to Christian, and he started smiling again. He wondered what he was doing now. Maybe he'd gone back to bed. He hadn't got much sleep the previous night. He was probably knackered, the poor man. Though he hadn't eaten either, maybe he'd gone in for breakfast at the hotel. Whatever he was doing, Harry had to forget him for a few hours and focus on the work ahead. They would be together soon enough, with an afternoon and a whole evening ahead of them.

Harry reached *The North Star*'s mooring point. There was no one on deck.

"Hey," he shouted down, "Tom. Your breakfast is here. Give me a hand, will you? I can't carry all this down the ladder."

He waited, and there was no answer.

"Tom," he shouted. Louder this time.

Still no reply. He must be below deck.

Harry tutted. He put the bag of food on the ground and carefully descended the slippery ladder one-handed with the coffee tray. Once it was set on the deck, he scooted back up to collect the carrier bag and brought that down, too.

"Hey," he called, "I thought you were hungry. Come and get it while it's still hot."

He flipped the lid off his own coffee cup and stirred in a sachet of brown sugar. It steamed, and he blew on the surface before taking a sip.

"Come on, Tom. Where are you?"

It struck him then that his cousin might be sick again. The bathroom on *The North Star* was on the lower deck, accessed through a hatch in the wheelhouse. Harry put the coffee down and crossed the deck. The light was on and as he stepped inside, time seemed to stop.

Tom was slumped in the corner of the cabin at an awkward angle. His legs were spread and jutted out in front of him. His torso was slumped sideways, supported by his bent right arm, the other arm laying at his side. His eyes were open, but the expression on his face was slack, his mouth gaped. He wore a navy sweater and light blue jeans. At first the blood was not obvious against the darkness of his sweater, but as Harry's disbelieving gaze wandered all over him, he saw it, staining the front of his jeans, spreading across the deck beneath.

Harry found his breath and screamed. The noise jolted him out of the paralysis.

"Tom."

He flung himself to the floor.

"Tom," he yelled again.

He gripped his shoulders, shaking him. His head fell to an even more bizarre angle. There was no response.

The blood. Where is it coming from?

Harry tore at his clothes, pulling up his sweater. His white T-shirt was wet with warm, deep scarlet fluid.

Harry peeled the cotton back to reveal the full horror beneath.

The cry that escaped him was a raw sound of grief and despair.

Chapter Seventeen

Christian heard the sirens while he was in the shower. They seemed to pass right below the window. *Just an average morning in Nyemouth*, he thought with a wry smile as he lathered his torso. For a small seaside town, it appeared that there was rarely a dull moment.

He thrust his head beneath the showerhead. The pressure of the water was wonderful, and he luxuriated in the heat. The chilly, fog-bound walk from Harry's place to the hotel seemed to have let the cold into his bones, but after a few minutes he felt normal again.

He was physically tired after an energetic night with Harry, but far too excited to sleep. He found himself smiling at nothing, even now, just thinking about Harry. The young man had brought an energy into his life that Christian hadn't experienced in years — maybe not for a decade. He was caught up in the rush of getting to know someone, of rapidly developing emotions. In ordinary circumstances, he might have put the brakes on about now. He believed in caution and taking his time, behaving sensibly. But right now, he didn't want to.

Just for once, he wanted to surrender to these sensations and see what came of them.

The mindful part of him was aware that he would be going back to Manchester in a little over a week, that it was foolish to form attachments so far from home. This morning, he didn't care about any of that. What he felt was wonderful, and he intended to enjoy it to the fullest.

He shut off the water, wiped himself down and stepped out of the shower. As he reached for a towel, he heard another siren blare past. Whatever was going on out there, it sounded like another Nyemouth emergency.

He glanced through the gap in the open window. The fog was clearing. It was more of a light mist now. *Oh, well. Harry will be taking his fishing charter out soon.* Christian couldn't grumble. It was Harry's livelihood. He couldn't give it up to spend the day with a passing tourist.

He towelled off, put on deodorant and fixed his hair. As he wandered into the bedroom, another siren flew by.

What the hell?

Christian opened the sash window as far as it would go and leaned out.

There was something going on in the harbour. He saw the lights of an ambulance and two police cars. He stretched farther out, aiming for a better view. The emergency vehicles were parked more or less where Harry moored his boat.

The feeling of cold returned, icy tendrils that crept rapidly through his body.

No.

Christian raced to the wardrobe, grabbing under-pants, socks, jeans and a shirt. It took him seconds to pull them all on. He hurriedly shoved his feet into shoes and ran for the door. He couldn't wait for the elevator. Going for the stairs, he bounded down, two or three steps at a time. His heart raced, but it had nothing to do with the physical exertion.

He was desperate to know that Harry was all right.

Christian's heart seemed to fill his throat. He feared the worst. There had been two murders already this week, and the first victim had died onboard *The North Star*. Had the killer returned to take revenge on the owner of the rescue boat? Was Harry more involved than they had imagined?

Christian couldn't think straight.

He reached the ground floor and raced across the reception, almost knocking over a couple who were in the process of checking out, barrelling out of the far entrance into the alley, which cut down the side of the hotel. He raced to the seafront without pausing then pounded along the harbour.

A crowd had already gathered around the ambulance and police cars. He spotted uniformed officers pushing them back, trying to set up a perimeter.

His heart grew even heavier. There had definitely been a major incident of some sort.

He grabbed the arm of the nearest person. A woman in her sixties. "What happened? What is it?"

She shook him off and took a cautious step back. "I don't know. They're saying there's been another stabbing."

His heart grew even colder. Christian pressed the back of his hand to his mouth. His breath came in ragged gasps. "Who? Who has been attacked?"

The woman, clearly alarmed, slipped ever farther away from him. He turned to someone else, a balding man in his thirties.

"Who is it? Do you know?"

"Don't have a clue, mate. I'm not from round here. I'm just on holiday."

Shit.

Christian pushed into the crowd, brutally elbowing people aside, ignoring their angry protests. Someone grabbed his collar and tried to hold him back. He shook them free, battling his way to the front. His panic had reached a dangerous level. He couldn't think of anything but Harry.

If something has happened to him... Oh God.

When he got to the front, the police had already set up a cordon to keep the crowd at bay. He grabbed the tape and tried to slide underneath. A uniformed constable stepped forward and grabbed him.

"Keep back," the PC shouted.

Christian struggled in his grip. "You don't understand. I need to get through."

"No one is getting through. Unless you want me to arrest you, you need to step back."

"Listen to me —"

The PC grabbed his arm and twisted it behind his back. Christian didn't even feel the pain.

"I said get back."

"My...my boyfriend is on that boat. I need to know what's happened to him."

The constable relaxed his grip a fraction but did not release him. "What do you know about this?"

Christian pointed with his free hand. "*The North Star*. That's Harry Renner's boat."

From this distance, he could see the police and paramedics moving about on the deck. His gaze darted rapidly back and forth, searching for Harry amid the confusion.

What the hell is happening down there?

He froze.

Two paramedics carried a stretcher out of the wheelhouse. There was figure strapped in beneath a white sheet. The sheet had been drawn above the figure's face.

Christian's knees went from under him. He dropped, but the policeman swung an arm around him and kept him from going down.

"Take it easy," the cop said, his tone a lot kinder this time.

"Oh my God. Who is that? What the fuck has happened?"

Still supporting him, the PC gestured for help. A second constable came over and took hold of Christian from the other side. Christian didn't want their help. He wanted to know what was happening on that boat. *Right now.* Who the hell was on the stretcher and why?

A second later, he got his answer when Harry stumbled out of the wheelhouse.

Oh, thank God.

Harry's skin was a ghastly shade of grey. His face was a mask of shock and horror. One of the officers on the boat was talking to him. Harry nodded blankly. His hands were red. So were the front of his clothes.

Oh fuck. That's blood. What the hell has happened now?

"I need to go down there," Christian pleaded with the police officers.

"Sorry, mate," the first cop said, his tone far kinder than it had been before. "You can't go on that boat. It's a crime scene now."

"Crime scene?" The words sounded so foreign, so strange. Christian shook his head in denial. If it wasn't Harry on the stretcher, then who was it? "This doesn't make sense. Where's Tom? What's happened to him?"

Christian's manic behaviour was drawing even more attention. All around, people murmured and speculated about what had happened.

"It's Tom Renner," a loud voice carried over the crowd.

Christian felt the ripples of interest all around him.

The second police officer raised the cordon. "Come on through. We need to get you away from here."

As he slowly began to pay more attention, he recognised the PC from Monday night. She'd been at the lifeboat station, taking statements after they'd returned with Niko's body. He checked her name badge—Probationary Constable Indina Shah.

"Can I see Harry?" he asked. "Just for a moment."

"Sorry. Not yet. No one can go on that boat until it's been cleared by forensics." She led him by the arm to a police van, shielding him from the curious onlookers.

"I just want to know that he's all right."

"As soon as it's possible, I'll see what I can do. You said you are in a relationship with the boat owner. Is that correct?"

"Yes. It's very recent. But...PC Shah, please tell me what happened here? Did someone attack Harry and Tom? Does it have anything to do with the murder of Niko Jasinski? You know we were the ones who found him on Monday?"

She narrowed her eyes, looking at him more closely. "You were there, too? Oh, yes, of course you were. I remember you now. In that case, I'm going to get someone else to speak to you. Stay here, and don't move."

After twenty minutes of waiting without being seen, Christian had had enough. There were even more police officers on the dock now, and it was impossible for him to get anywhere near Harry or the boat. He spotted a bunch of fishermen on the other side of the cordon and recognised more than half of them from around the lifeboat station and the town. They might not know much, but something was better than nothing. Christian went over to them.

"Do any of you know what's happened?"

One of the older men stepped forward. "I was getting my boat ready so we could sail as soon as the fog lifted when I heard this God-awful scream from *The North Star*. It was young Harry calling for help. I knew straight away that something bad had gone down, especially after all that's gone on this week. I thought to myself, oh Lord, here's another one."

"What happened, though? The police won't tell me anything."

The fisherman looked grim. "It's Tom. Harry's cousin. Harry came back from fetching their breakfast and found him in the wheelhouse all cut up, just like those other two lads."

Christian folded his arms across his stomach and shook his head. He glanced over his shoulder, towards the boat. Harry was still on the deck. The police had not released him yet. He turned back to the fisherman and tried to speak, but there were no words.

"I don't know what's become of this town," the man said. "It used to be such a nice place to live. Now it seems like no one is safe anymore."

Chapter Eighteen

Harry arrived home after ten, almost twelve hours after he'd left the house that morning. It seemed like longer. How was it possible for so much shit to have gone down in a single day?

His parents had argued against him going back on his own, pleading with him to spend the night with them, but he needed to do it. There was a real and terrible possibility that he might never set foot on the deck of his boat again. He couldn't risk losing his home, too. Harry was afraid he might quit Nyemouth entirely after what had happened today.

The flat was emptier than he had even known when he closed the front door behind him and turned on the lights. The cosy living room and kitchen were cold. This morning's washed-up coffee cups stood on the drainer. The wall clocked ticked gently. There was his kettle, microwave and toaster. So many familiar items, but they didn't stop him from feeling like he'd walked into an alien environment.

The urge to run threatened to engulf him. He could turn right around and go back to his parents, but Harry knew that if he did that, there might be no return.

He pulled his phone from the pocket of the grey jogging bottoms the police had given him. All his own clothes were in their evidence bags. They'd provide him with the cheap trousers, a sweater and a pair of plain black sneakers at the station. The washing label in the sweater was stiff and grazed his skin. The fucking thing had been irritating him all afternoon. He rived the top over his shoulders and tossed it on the floor by the back door. He would burn it in the morning, along with the rest of this shit.

Turning back to his phone, he dialled Christian's number. He answered on the third ring.

"Harry." Christian didn't try to hide the urgency in his voice. "Thank God. How are you? Where are you?"

"I'm at home. I just got in. I…" He clutched the worktop, his eyes roamed around the room, and he didn't know what he wanted to say. "Can you come around?"

"I'll be right there."

"Thanks," he said, relieved. "Just give me ten minutes or so. I've got to get out of these clothes. Take a shower."

"I'll come for half-past. Is that okay?"

He exhaled, leaning against the counter. "Perfect. And, Christian…be careful."

"Don't worry. I'll see you soon."

Don't worry. That was an impossibility.

Harry kicked off the awful shoes and slipped down the joggers. He threw them in a heap at the back door and went along to the bathroom. He avoided his reflection as he waited for the water to heat up. He didn't want to see how bad he looked. The pain inside was awful enough. He didn't need to see it etched across his face.

He climbed into the stall and shoved his head beneath the faucet. He grabbed the shower gel and lathered up his body, keeping his eyes closed. If there was any residue of Tom's blood remaining on his body or in his hair, he didn't want to see it swirl around the drain. He kept a nail brush in the shower to help scrub the smell of fish and diesel from his hands. Harry located it by touch and attacked his nails with blind fury, scouring until the tips of his fingers were raw.

When he left the shower and vigorously rubbed himself with a clean towel, it did not seem enough. After all he had done, he did not feel clean. He wondered if he ever would again.

It seemed unlikely.

He put on a pair of lounge pants and a T-shirt and was combing his damp hair when there was a knock at the front door. He hurried to answer, falling into Christian's embrace when he opened it. Christian, holding a shopping bag, still managed to hug him the way he needed.

"It's okay," Christian whispered, pressing his face against Harry's neck. "I'm here."

Harry's eyes prickled with tears. He'd thought he was cried out. Crying. He felt it was all he had done today. His tear ducts were raw. Christian held him for over a minute before guiding him inside. He locked the door behind them.

Harry let out a humourless snort. "The police told me I should be careful, not to take any risks, and I answered that door without even checking who was there."

"You'll remember next time," Christian said, following him to the kitchen.

Jesus. This time last night they'd sat in this very room enjoying their takeaway dinner with little to worry about. It frightened him how quickly things could change.

Christian emptied the bag onto the table. There was a bottle of Scotch. "I figured you might need something strong," he said. He produced a loaf of bread and a packet of pre-cooked chicken breast. "And food. Have you eaten?"

Harry shook his head. "I had a couple of biscuits at my parent's house. My mam kept plying us with tea. I feel like I've got it coming out of my ears."

Christian stroked the side of his face. "Sit. Let me fix you something. If you only eat a few mouthfuls, it will do you good."

"Okay. Thanks. I wanted to speak to you earlier. I saw you at the station, but there was no opportunity." He fetched two tumblers from a cupboard, sat at the table and set about opening the whisky.

"You were gone by the time they took my statement," Christian said. "I think they wanted to keep us apart until they got the facts from each of us, just to be sure our stories matched."

"Do you think they suspect us? Suspect me of murdering my own cousin?" Anger rose in his throat.

"They are just doing their job." Christian spoke softly, placing a light hand on Harry's shoulder. "For Tom's sake, you don't want them to cut corners. I don't think they suspect you at all, but they have to consider every option." He opened several cupboards until he located a chopping board. "Is it okay if I raid the fridge?

I went to that convenience store in the marina, but they didn't have a lot left."

Harry nodded. He pulled the cork out of the whisky bottle and splashed a good inch into each tumbler. "How do you take this?"

"With water. I'll get it."

Christian took another glass and filled it from the tap. He brought it to the table and splashed a little into his whisky, about a third as much as spirit. Harry did the same and sipped while Christian opened the fridge. The liquor was strong with a warm heat that soothed his throat as he swallowed, and it warmed his stomach.

Harry released a sad sigh. "I suppose they have every right to suspect us. Three young lads have been murdered inside of a week, and we were the last people to see *two* of them alive."

Christian rinsed a handful of cherry tomatoes and put them on the chopping board. "The idea had occurred to me, too, and, from the point of view of the police, it makes sense for them to suspect us. But something worries me far more than being a person of interest in their investigation. What if you're not so much a suspect as a target?"

"Really?"

"The thought has been going round my mind all day until I've convinced myself it was the only answer — that whoever came after Tom did so because of what happened on the boat on Monday. And if you had been there this morning, they might have attacked you, too."

Harry took another sip, avoiding the concern in Christian's eyes. "It's a struggle to accept that," he said at last. "Niko was half dead when we pulled him from the sea. He didn't say a word. He couldn't tell us what happened or who attacked him. We don't know any more than the police do about his attacker."

Christian peeled the skin off the chicken breasts and cut them into thick slices. "The killer doesn't know that. They might be out there wondering whether you do know something and if you're keeping the information to yourself for now."

"Why would I? That's insane."

"I know, but so is the person behind all this. They have to be. Maybe they've been stewing on the idea all week, and by this morning had convinced themselves it must be true. They couldn't take the risk of us talking, so decided to do something about it." Christian knocked off his drink in one slug and brought the empty glass back to the table, eyeing the bottle for a refill. "That's what I told the police today, anyway."

Harry drained his own glass and topped them both up. "Did they think it was plausible?"

He screwed up his face. "I don't think so. They told me that we should be careful — like you said before, not to take any unnecessary risks. But I don't think they saw it as a logical theory — no more than the two of us being killers, anyway."

He returned to the counter to finish making the sandwiches.

Harry swirled the liquor around his glass, gazing at the light amber colours. "It's a pretty fucked-up motive. I don't know whether I *don't* believe it or don't *want* to believe it. It seems like such a stretch, that's all. Unreal. But so does everything else right now. *Fuck.*"

"Do you want anything else on here? Beetroot? Mayo? Mustard?"

"A little mayo. Thanks."

Christian finished the sandwiches, cut them in two, and brought the plates to the table. He sat beside Harry, and Harry looked at him gratefully. He picked one up and took a bite. His mouth was dry, and it was a struggle to chew at first, until he realised just how hungry he was.

"How is Tom's family? He had one kid, right?"

Harry swallowed and nodded. He cleared his throat. "Joshua. He's four. The poor lad doesn't even know what has happened. Susan's sister, Paula, has taken him. She lives down the coast in Newbiggin. It's probably for the best to get him away from it all. Susan is devastated. Her parents are staying with her, but she didn't know whether she was coming or going when I saw her. I don't know if she'll ever get over it."

Christian nodded sympathetically.

A sudden gust rattled the back door, and they both started. Christian got up and went straight to the window, peering out into the dark. "Just the wind," he muttered and sat back down. "I guess what the police said has got us both spooked."

"The weather is supposed to turn nasty again tonight. Tomorrow looks as bad as Monday. I reckon you're right. I must be spooked, because this kind of thing doesn't usually bother me."

They finished their sandwiches in silence before Christian reached across the table and took his hand. "This is probably a stupid question, but do you have any weapons in the house?"

"Of course not. I'm a fisherman, not a hunter."

The corners of Christian's mouth turned downwards. "I thought as much." He got up and opened the drawers. Rummaging through, he pulled out a long butcher's knife and a carving knife. He ran his fingers along the blade and frowned, before shuffling through the drawers again until he found a knife sharpener. "This will do," he said, drawing the first blade back and forth across the sharpening rod.

Harry let out a weary laugh. "You do know that we're not allowed to carry knives around in this country, not even for protection."

"There are no laws against having them in your own home." Christian put the first knife on the table in front of him. "Keep this with you wherever you are, even when you go to the bathroom."

"Aren't you overacting?"

"Do you really need to ask that question? After today?"

"I suppose not."

After clearing up, they carried the whisky bottle and their knives into the living room. Harry turned on the gas fire and they settled on the sofa. He lay full stretch with his head resting on Christian's thigh. Christian trailed his fingertips through his hair, softly curling it around.

"Do you want to tell me what happened this morning?" Christian asked. "You don't have to if you've had enough. I'll understand. I was able to fill in the pieces from what the police said."

Harry gazed up at his face. The flames from the fire illuminated him in casts of amber and gold. "I've gone over it so many times today that once more won't hurt."

He told it all again, sticking to facts in a plain, almost mechanical manner. Returning to the boat with breakfast, calling out for Tom, finding him in the cabin. He had recounted the story so often that it felt like just that, a story. It played more like a movie in his head than reality, everything but the final shot — that awful discovery of his cousin's body. The sight of Tom slumped in the wheelhouse, lifeless and mutilated, would stay seared in his mind for the rest of his life.

"Darling, I'm so sorry." Christian ran his fingers down the side of his face and over his neck to his chest. He rested his hand gently above Harry's heart. Harry lifted his own hand, put it on top of his and neither of them spoke again for a long time.

They finally went to bed around three-thirty. Christian checked the flat from front to back, ensuring that all the doors and windows were locked. Harry was exhausted, but when he climbed beneath the covers, he had no expectation of sleep. There was too much going on in his mind. Harry slid in next to him and Christian curled onto his side, spooned in Christian's protective embrace.

The sharpened knives were on the tables on either side of the bed.

Harry closed his eyes and was asleep in less than a minute.

Chapter Nineteen

Christian woke to the sound of wind gusting along the side of the house. As his senses stirred, he perceived the roar of the sea close by, waves crashing against the harbour walls. Harry had rolled onto his stomach during the night, facing away from him. His breath was deep and even. Christian turned slowly, careful not to disturb him, and picked up his watch from the bedside table. It was eight-forty-two.

His head was heavy from last night's whisky, and his mouth was dry and bitter.

With even greater care, he slipped out of bed and walked on the balls of his feet to the bathroom down the hall. He'd discovered during his visits here that the noisy floorboards declared every step and movement. Christian relieved himself, then ran the cold tap and gulped from his cupped hand until his booze-induced thirst was quenched.

When he returned to the bedroom, Harry lay on his back, propped on one arm behind his head.

"What time is it?" he asked.

"Never mind that," Christian told him. "Go back to sleep. You need it." He slipped under the covers.

"I'm awake now."

"How do you feel?"

He sighed. "Okay. Still numb but rested. I didn't expect to sleep at all, but I must have. I don't remember waking during the night."

"You needed it." Christian edged closer to his warm body and slid an arm across his chest.

"I half-hoped as I started to pull around that yesterday was nothing more than a nightmare, a delirious cheese-dream. It didn't last long before reality kicked in hard."

"You've had a massive shock on top of all the other stress you've been under. It will take time for you to adjust. Try not to force it."

"So, what time is it?"

"Almost nine."

"Christ. I haven't slept that late in years, not since I was a teenager."

"It was a late night."

"I need to get moving."

"Stay here a little longer. The rest will do you good."

"I'd love to, but I've already made plans to meet my family this morning. If I'm late, they'll send a search party down here looking for me, if not the entire Nyemouth police force."

A stab of disappointment hit Christian in the stomach, but he kept it to himself. He wanted to spend the day with Harry, to watch over and protect him — to prevent any further harm from coming to him. He knew he was being selfish. It was natural that Harry's family wanted to do the same thing. He, a stranger, couldn't stand in the way of that.

"Come with me," Harry said. He turned onto his side. "I mean it. You could be in danger, too, if your theory about Tom's killer is true. You shouldn't be alone."

He ran his hand across Harry's bare shoulder. "As much as I appreciate it, I'm not ready to meet your folks quite yet."

"But—"

"I'll be fine. Don't worry. I won't be alone. I'll call Dominic and Arnie and ask if I can spend the day with them. I won't take any risks. I promise."

"Can I see you later?"

"Try to keep me away."

While Harry took a shower, Christian put on a pot of coffee. He checked his phone while waiting for it to brew, hoping there might have been some new developments overnight. Nothing. He checked the BBC website, local newsgroups and Nyemouth social media pages and drew a blank on all of them. Whoever was responsible for the murders of Niko, Ike, and now Tom, was still out there.

Christian shoved his phone in his back pocket when Harry returned, fully dressed.

"I was going to fix you some cereal," he said with a smile, "but your cupboards are bare."

"That's because I usually get breakfast in town. It will have to be toast." Harry retrieved a loaf from the freezer and dropped two slices into the toaster.

Christian stepped behind him and wrapped his arms around him, snuggling in. "Please be careful today. I'm scared of anything happening to you."

Harry put both hands on Christian's arms. "That goes both ways. Don't take any risks, eh? Get a taxi up to Dominic's if he can't come to collect you."

"Deal." He kissed the side of Harry's neck and breathed in the soapy scent of his skin and hair. He wanted to hold the memory of every part of him until they met again that night.

* * * *

"Hey, Manchester," a voice hollered at him across the marina.

Christian was on the steps outside his hotel. He turned. A familiar-looking woman in a red parka hurried towards him. His head was still heavy from the whisky, and it took a moment to realise who she was — Marie Baxter-Booth, the local TV news reporter. He suppressed a groan. He was still wearing last night's clothes and was desperate for a shower. The hotel was only a few minutes' walk from Harry's place. All he wanted was to freshen up and change before heading up to Dominic's. Answering questions from the press was the last thing he wanted.

"Ms. Baxter-Booth, I bet you didn't expect to be back here so soon." Impatience was clear in his tone.

"There's an understatement. We might as well set up a permanent office here." She stood on the steps below him, fixing him with a direct stare. Strong winds buffered them. "You lied to me."

His shoulders sagged, and he looked away, towards the far side of the river. The doors of the lifeboat station were open. He remembered Dominic saying how they often carried out training exercises on Sunday mornings. Looking at the state of the sea, he doubted they would go out today, not unless an emergency came up.

"I asked you if you were on the boat with Niko Jasinski on Monday. You said no."

He looked back at her. "That's right."

Wind whipped her hair across her face, and she swiped it aside. "Why? You're a journalist. Why would you pull such a shitty trick?"

"Because it wasn't something I wanted to talk about out of respect for the family, for the victim, because some things are more important than a story. Are they good enough reasons, or do you want me to go on?"

"Don't give me that bullshit. And don't try to tell me you didn't know the latest victim, either — the guy who died on the very boat you were on."

"Well, it seems you've got your story already. You don't need me. Now, this is no morning to stand around chatting. Excuse me."

"Hold on," she barked. "You owe me, as one professional to another."

He stifled a laugh. "Good one. That's not how it works, I'm afraid." He took another step towards the door.

"Wait. I probably know more about this than you do. I've got contacts within the police. They are talking. Now, if you tell me your side of the story, I'll fill you in on what I know. C'mon. Surely that's an offer you can't refuse."

He sighed. "All right, come inside. Let's at least get out of this lousy weather."

He took her into the hotel bar and ordered two coffees. There were no other customers at that time of day, but they took the table the greatest distance from the counter to ensure they had privacy. Marie removed her puffer jacket to reveal a warm sweater underneath.

"Not broadcasting today?" he asked.

"Only if the story breaks. I've got a suit and blouse on standby in the car if I need it." She used her fingers to comb out the short tangles in her hair.

"Are the police that close to a breakthrough? To making an arrest?"

"You're kidding, aren't you? These plods... The killer will have to walk through the door of the station and put himself in cuffs before they get close to catching them."

"Harsh, but I dare say you're right." The experience he'd had at Nyemouth station yesterday had instilled little faith. The local police were woefully out of their depths.

"There's a major incident team moving in tomorrow." Marie looked pleased with herself, proving already that she knew more than he did. "They'll take over from the Nyemouth flatfoots, so maybe there will be some developments soon...or maybe not."

"So, what else do you know?"

Marie shook her head. "You first. You're the one who has been involved since the first day. I want to know your story."

"I'm not going to disrespect the victims for the benefit of your feature. I'll tell you about my own experiences on the boat—what I saw, how I felt—but that's as far as it goes."

Marie tightened her mouth.

"That's as good as it gets. If you want to know about Niko and Tom, it's for their families to tell you. And if they don't want to, that's just tough."

Her stare was hard and challenging. Christian did not back down and faced her out.

"Oh, all right," she said at last. "Tell me your side."

He told about his reasons for coming to Nyemouth, how he had chartered the boat as part of his research trip and the sudden change in the weather while they were at sea. He told her about spotting something in the water on the way back and raising the alarm — about the sickness, anxiety and fear he had experienced since, only pausing when their coffee was delivered.

"And yesterday?" she asked. "Tom Renner?"

"I wasn't there," he answered truthfully. "I was here. Upstairs, taking a shower when I heard the sirens. I only found out what had happened to him when I went along the harbour to investigate."

"The police questioned you?"

"Yes. I saw Tom for a few seconds first thing in the morning, while he was setting up the boat for their next trip. That's all."

Marie looked unimpressed. "I still get the feeling you're holding out on me."

"I am, but I've given you the reasons why. I won't go into the grisly details of what I saw. Now, it's your turn."

She frowned, as though giving serious thought to the idea of telling him to fuck off, then her expression softened. "Okay. Seeing as you're not actually reporting on this story… The police haven't confirmed this officially, but I know that laptops and mobile phones are missing from both Niko and Ike Meekers."

"Robbery?" he suggested.

"For Ike, maybe. And if it was just the phone, that would be true for Niko, too. But someone broke into his house and took the laptop — nothing else, just that. And it most likely happened immediately after he was attacked."

"So, there's something on the laptop they don't want anyone else knowing about. Any ideas."

Marie raised the coffee cup to her mouth with both hands and sipped. "They are looking at all options —

fraud, blackmail, porn. Have you heard of websites like OnlyFans?"

Christian hid his excitement. *So, my theory wasn't that far out.* "Sure."

"Well, I understand that's one of the lines of enquiry. Niko was a content creator on numerous sites of that type, only the cops don't know what yet. They know he had accounts but not the name he posted under, and the sites haven't been forthcoming with the information—data protection and all that. The cops need a court order, but that could take days."

"Haven't any of his friends been able to tell them his username?"

"No. He'd confided in a few of them about his accounts. Apparently, he was earning a nice amount of extra cash per month, but he didn't tell anyone his ID. It makes sense. Who wants their friends checking out their online sex work, eh?"

He thought about Gemma Payne and the sex clips she had found on Niko's phone. Maybe she had drawn the wrong conclusion after all, and the girls on Niko's phone were other models rather than his girlfriends. He wasn't about to tell Marie what he knew. It was too personal. Gemma didn't need to hear the theory on the early evening news.

"And what about Ike Meeker?" he asked. "Any connection to online sex work?"

"Not that I'm aware of. He wasn't really the type. You know, a little overweight, kind of average looking."

"Beauty is in the eye of the beholder," he said. "What's unattractive to one person is a turn-on to another."

"It's possible. He could have been posting stuff online, but I haven't heard anything to suggest it yet."

"Why take his laptop, then? What's the connection?"

Marie's expression darkened. "I don't fucking know. Maybe there isn't one. Maybe it was a robbery, pure and simple."

"I've not heard anything about Tom's phone or computer being stolen, either," he said. "So, there's even less to connect him than the first two."

"Apart from his participation in the rescue of Niko Jasinski...just like you." Her eyes bore into his.

"The thought has already occurred to me," he told her. "Is that it, then? Cause it doesn't sound like you know more than anyone else. Gossips about town have been spouting the OnlyFans theory for most of the week, but it doesn't fit with the other murders."

"All right, smart arse. Well, I don't know how much you know about these fan-based porn sites, but I always thought it was people charging for their naked selfies and nudie pics. Apparently, that's amateur time. The serious content creators, and the ones who make the biggest money, are the most professional. They use proper photographers and beautiful models to film their stuff, usually in posh hotels or studios."

His eyes widened. "So, someone could know what he was filming and with whom?"

Marie grinned. "Exactly. If he made as much money as people are saying he did, there is every chance Niko hired a professional photographer, and that person knows something about his secret life."

* * * *

Antoni had sent several texts to Harry in the last twenty-four hours, none of which had been answered.

He didn't bear a grudge, not after what Harry had been through. Antoni wouldn't be surprised to learn he had switched his phone off completely. Following Tom's murder, Nyemouth was once again buzzing with talk of serial killers.

Antoni had spent the morning at the gallery, and it was all anyone who came in wanted to talk about.

Have you heard what happened? Do you know any of the victims?

The gale force winds coming from the sea, with even worse conditions forecast for this evening, would usually have kept the tourists away, but the gallery had seen its busiest morning since the summer heights of July and August. Murder, it seemed, was great for business.

Antoni had answered the questions with a non-committal shake of his head. He would not pander to the morbid thrill seekers. They would draw their own conclusions, anyway.

He was more concerned about Harry. His ex-boyfriend was a tough one. It took a lot to get him down. He had barely turned a head when they'd broken up after all their years together. Harry didn't allow his emotions to get in the way of his work. But this was different. He and Tom had always been close. His cousin's death was bound to have hit him hard.

Antoni was desperate to talk to him. Even if he had the writer to comfort him, what good could a man like that be? He was a stranger. They had known each other for less than a week.

That man couldn't help Harry the way Antoni could.

When Roger took over the gallery at one p.m., Antoni grabbed his coat.

"You're going out in this?" Roger questioned.

"It's still dry, despite the wind. I need some air to clear my head. You'll be all right. Things have quietened down a lot." Which was true. The tourist trade had slackened off around midday. They had no doubt got bored with the lack of news and had disappeared to the pubs or gone home to stuff their faces with Sunday lunch.

The streets were quiet as he crossed the bridge to the North Side. The wind was cold and strong in his face, though the rain was not due until later this afternoon. The conditions at sea were wild. Beyond the pier heads, he could see tumultuous waves crashing on the shore. That would only get worse at high tide this evening.

When he arrived at Harry's door, Antoni was unsure of what to say if his new boyfriend answered. He hoped it wouldn't come to that and knocked before he changed his mind. When there was no answer, he knocked again then walked along to the front window. The living room was empty. There were no lights on. No TV.

Damn.

He should have known he wouldn't be there. Harry was probably with Tom's wife or his parents.

Antoni knew where they lived, but he couldn't go there. What he had to say could not be done in front of others.

He checked his phone again. Still no answer to his texts. *Shit.* With no other options, he dialled Harry's number. After several rings, it went to voicemail.

Antoni's heart was in his throat when he spoke. "Hi, it's me. I need to speak to you quite urgently. I need to talk to you before anyone else. It's about Tom. There's something you should know."

Chapter Twenty

Harry bowed his head as he battled directly into the wind blowing down Pier Street. It was currently raging at around forty miles per hour, with gusts of more than fifty. If the forecast were correct, they would see speeds of ninety to a hundred this evening. Harry intended to be warm and cosy indoors by then, hopefully with Christian.

He wouldn't be out now if he hadn't received the mysterious message from Antoni. He had intended to stay with his parents until later afternoon before making his way to Quay House to meet Christian. Antoni hadn't answered when he had returned the call. *What the hell did it mean?* Antoni and Tom knew each other through him, but they had never been more than casual acquaintances. Though they had been together a few years, Harry hadn't made a big thing of introducing Antoni to his family. He had always kept his personal life very separate.

Antoni might have exchanged words with Tom if they'd run into him in one of the pubs or maybe in the

Seagull, but Harry hadn't been aware of anything more meaningful than that between them. He couldn't remember either of them speaking to him about the other.

The Northumberland Gallery closed at four on Sundays. It had gone half-three, so if Antoni wouldn't answer his phone, Harry figured it was as good a place as any to speak to him.

It was a relief to step out of the bracing wind into the entrance. The gallery was really just two rooms. The back area was where the brothers displayed their art – Roger's painting and Antoni's photographs – while out front they had a small shop where they sold cheaper prints and reproductions, together with the usual gift shop fare of notebooks, pencils, badges and postcards.

Roger was at the counter when he went inside.

"Harry," he said, looking up, surprised. Roger immediately came around to the front with open arms. His embrace was firm and welcome. "I'm so sorry about Tom. How are you doing?"

"Thank you. Okay, I guess. I'm not really sure, to be honest. I don't think it has sunk in."

Roger stepped back. There was genuine concern on his face. "That's only natural. I don't think anyone has got to grips with what's gone on this week. It's been so crazy. I only knew Tom a little. I spoke to him a few times in the club. He was always there when there was a Newcastle match on. He loved his football."

Emotions surged once again. Whenever he spoke to someone new about Tom, his feelings threatened to overwhelm him. Harry swallowed the knot in his throat. "Yeah, he did. I didn't know what he was talking about most of the time, but it didn't stop him from going on about it."

"He had the bug. He was a nice man. He will be greatly missed, I'm sure."

Harry nodded, looking at the floor until the impending tears were under control. "Is Antoni around? He left me a message. Said he wanted to talk."

"No, he's out," Roger said. "He's gone along to the pier with his camera. He wanted to take pictures of the storm before it gets dark. He gets some crazy ideas at times, though when I looked out earlier, it was very dramatic. He should get some good shots."

"Ah, okay. I might have a look along that way and see if he's still there."

"You can wait here if you like. I'll make some coffee. It will be a lot more comfortable."

"Thanks. I appreciate the offer, but I could do with the fresh air. These strong winds might help to clear my head."

Roger gave an understanding nod. "Well, take care of yourself. And please give my regards to Tom's wife and his family. I'm deeply sorry for your loss."

Harry thanked him again and went outside.

Pier Street was empty. At the height of summer, he would have struggled to cross the road for the crowds of tourists streaming in both directions. It was always a little eerie at this time of year, more so in the dark — or maybe it was just him dwelling on morbid thoughts because of Tom.

Harry remembered the warning he'd been given by Christian and the police about taking precautions. It probably wasn't the best idea to be up here on his own. Then again, did he really believe he was in danger? *Probably not.* The suggestion that Niko's killer might be seeking revenge on the people who had tried to rescue him was the stuff of horror films, not reality.

Harry wasn't taking any unnecessary risks. He would walk as far as the pier. If Antoni was there, then he wouldn't be alone, anyway. They could come back together. If he wasn't, then he'd turn around and make his way to Quay House. Besides, it wouldn't get dark for a couple of more hours yet.

At the end of Pier Street, the road narrowed to a steep footpath. There was no shelter from the wind now as he followed the course upwards, along the base of the cliff, until he reached the bank which led to the pier. The sea was wild, a seething grey mass with waves of twenty to thirty feet crashing against the shore. The sky was battleship grey with more ominous black clouds on the far horizon.

Harry stood for a moment, losing himself in the dramatic spectacle, filling his lungs with air and taking the full force of the wind in his face. He would hate to be out there on his boat right now, but from the safety of land, this was breath-taking. He had always had an appreciation of nature and a respect for it. Most people who made their living at sea were the same. It was madness not to.

The waves battered the lower level of the pier, but they weren't high enough to reach the top tier. Not yet, but by high tide at five-thirty, he was sure they would.

He scanned the landscape for signs of Antoni and spotted a figure in a red waterproof below.

Harry pulled the zipper of his jacket up to his chin and set off down the bank towards him.

* * * *

Christian loaded empty plates into the dishwasher.

"Hey, you don't need to do that," Arnie said. "You're a guest. Sit back down."

"Don't be daft. I want to help. You should sit and let me do this."

Arnie raised his hands in surrender. "Okay, if you insist." He poured a cup of coffee and pulled out a chair at the kitchen table.

Christian had been up at the house for most of the afternoon with Arnie, his son AJ and AJ's friend Karim. The two boys were now in the living room playing video games. Dominic was still at the lifeboat station for their regular Sunday training. When Christian had called earlier and discovered he wouldn't be home, he was about to change his plans, but Arnie had insisted he come for lunch, anyway. "You'll be doing me a huge favour," Arnie had said, explaining that AJ had a friend staying over. "I'm desperate for some adult company."

It had been a pleasant relief for Christian, too. With the two youngsters around, all talk of murder and suspicion had been quashed. It had allowed him to focus on something else for a few hours, even if it was school achievements and football.

When the dishwasher was loaded and the benches were all clear, he poured himself a cup of coffee and sat across from Arnie. For a famous actor, there was nothing grand or mighty about Arnie. He was a very grounded and unassuming guy.

"How is it going with Harry?" he asked. "Still good? I mean, apart from all the shit that's going down."

Christian snorted softly. "Great, I would say, apart from the shit. He's the nicest guy I've ever met. It's early days and I guess we don't really know each other that well, but I have a positive feeling about him. It's just" — he gave an exasperated sigh — "all this craziness. I can't begin to imagine what things will be like afterwards."

Arnie folded his arms on the table and leaned closer. "If it's meant to be, it will be fine. I promise you, with whatever happens. Dominic and me? We didn't get together at the best of times, either. On the night we first met, AJ and I witnessed an attempted murder, right out there on the point." He jerked his thumb to the front window. "And a few days later, my own life was at risk. If it hadn't been for Dominic and AJ, I wouldn't be here now. To say we met at a bad time is putting it mildly. But it all worked out in the end. I'm sure it will for you, too."

"You guys are perfect. I can't see how anything could have stopped you from getting together. You were made for each other."

"It will be the same for you and Harry," Arnie said assuredly. "If that's what you both want."

Christian grinned. "I'd like that. I really would."

Dominic came home a few minutes later. When he opened the kitchen door, a powerful gust of wind came through and it was an effort for him to close the door behind him.

"Wow," he said, smoothing down his windswept hair. "What a day. I hope I don't have to go back out in that."

He came to the table and leaned over. Arnie turned and raised his head and they kissed briefly.

"There's a plate for you in the fridge," Arnie said. "It'll just need heating through."

"I'm fine for now. I think I ate my weight in biscuits down at the station." Dominic turned to Christian. "I'm glad you're still here. I take it you haven't heard the latest news?"

Christian sat up straight. "What news?"

"I thought not," Dominic said, taking off his coat. "We only heard ourselves about an hour ago. The police are looking for Reece Wallace. They think he had something to do with the murders. Well, Niko's and Tom's at least."

"What?" Christian said.

Arnie turned his chair to look straight at Dominic. "Reece Wallace? The fisherman's son?"

Dominic nodded. "That's right. Stew Wallace's kid."

"But he's only a child."

"Eighteen."

"Hang on," Christian said. "Reece? I think that's the boy who helped Harry the other day, when Tom was sick."

"Yeah," Dominic said. "That's right. He did."

"Shit," Arnie drawled. "So why? What makes them think it's him?"

"It's all hearsay at the minute, but he was seen arguing with Tom outside The Lobster Pot last week. It got pretty heated, if what they're saying is true. And Niko's old girlfriend, Gemma, has told the police that him and Reece had fallen out over something, too."

"It could be anything," Arnie said. "It doesn't make him a killer."

Dominic raised his eyebrows. "Darling, you have a short memory. You know better than anyone what certain people are capable of. There has to be something in it if the cops are hunting for him. They were down by the marina earlier, checking over Stew's boat. I saw them myself, straight across the river from the station."

Christian stiffened. "So, he's not in custody? He's still out there?"

"Yeah."

Christian leapt to his feet. "I have to warn Harry. If he came for Tom, he could go after him, too." He dialled the number, pacing the floor while he waited for an answer.

When Harry picked up, Christian couldn't hear anything but static and roaring wind.

"...ello," Harry said.

"Hey. Can you hear me?"

"...eally hard...what...aying?"

"Harry, where are you?"

The reply was garbled. Harry's voice was lost in the wind and the terrible connection.

Christian's pulse pounded in his temples. "I don't know if you can hear me, but you need to be careful. Stay away from Reece Wallace. Did you get that? Reece Wallace. He's wanted by the police."

The line went dead.

"Fuck!"

"What is it?" Dominic asked.

"Shitty connection. It sounded like he was in a wind tunnel. I don't think he could hear me, either."

Arnie was on his feet. "Send a text. He should get that wherever he is."

Christian hurriedly composed the message.

Reece Wallace is trouble. Police want him for murder. If you see him, stay away.

His hands shook as he hit Send. "Damn, this isn't good enough. What if he doesn't get it?"

"We don't know for sure that Reece will go after Harry," Arnie said.

"Yes," Dominic added. "And if he knows the police are after him, there's a good chance he's left town. He's probably miles away from here."

Their words could not quell the terror that gnawed at his insides. Harry was in danger. He was certain of it.

Christian wouldn't relax until he knew Harry was safe.

He had to take action.

Chapter Twenty-One

"I can't really hear what you're saying," Harry shouted. He turned his back to the wind, and his head away from it, but it was no good. All he could make out was static. "I'm out by the south pier. The reception is terrible. I'll call you back in twenty minutes or so." He hung up and shoved the phone into his coat pocket.

Christian was probably calling to find out where he was and arrange a time for them to meet. As soon as he was finished with Antoni, Harry would track him down.

Antoni was about halfway out on the pier. He didn't appear to have noticed Harry's arrival. His camera was pointed towards North Point, no doubt capturing some strong images as the waves smashed against the jagged rocks beneath the cliff. Harry shoved his hands in his pockets for warmth and headed towards him.

Waves pounded the base of piers and washed over the lower tier. In an hour from now, he reckoned it would not be safe to walk on. At least the rain had held off. He hoped it continued until he was in the warmth of Quay House or The Fisherman's Arms.

"Antoni," he shouted as he got nearer, but his words were carried away on the wind blowing in the wrong direction. Harry strengthened his stance and battled on.

Antoni turned and saw him when he was less than twenty feet away.

"Are you mad?" Harry hollered. "What the hell are you doing out on an afternoon like this? And here, of all places."

Antoni raised his camera. "I think these are going to be amazing. Roger may even want to use them for one of his paintings." He pointed in the direction of North Beach. "I don't think I've even taken anything so remarkable. The light, those clouds, the sea. Everything is just about perfect." He sounded strangely exhilarated and oblivious to the mounting danger.

"You'll need to turn back soon," Harry said, siding up to him. "There's a real chance the waves are going to wash over the top."

"I'm about done." He raised the camera and fired off some more shots.

"What's this about Tom?" Harry asked. "I got your message, but I don't understand."

Antoni continued clicking before finally lowering the camera and looking at him. His expression was deadly serious. He inhaled and exhaled through his mouth. "I didn't want it to come out this way, but I was awake most of last night turning things over. I'm going to speak to the police this evening, but I want to tell you first." He shook his head and walked to the edge of the pier. He gripped the railing and stared upriver towards the town. "Shit. I should have spoken to them earlier. If I had, maybe Tom would have…"

What the hell is this? Harry followed and stood beside him. "Do you know something about what happened to Tom?"

Another low exhalation. "I don't know. I thought not. Tried to convince myself it had nothing to do with Niko's death. That it would only upset his parents if I mentioned it and they have suffered enough." He paused again, seeming to struggle for words.

"For God's sake, what is it? Antoni, come on, tell me. I'm starting to worry here."

His knuckles whitened as he gripped the rail harder.

"Niko was making money on the side. Online. He was producing…sex tapes and selling them. Oh, I don't know exactly how it works. It's like an adult social media account. People paid to follow him, and he uploaded videos of himself."

So, the rumours are true. "OnlyFans, you mean? That kind of thing?"

Antoni shrugged and stared at the sea. "I don't know what he called it. I think there is more than one. Niko approached me about it last year quite matter-of-factly. I think he was proud of it. He asked if I would film some new content for him. He was going to have sex with a couple of women from Newcastle and wanted me to shoot them in a professional way. Of course, I refused. My God, I've known him since he was a boy. I didn't want to see all that."

Harry frowned. "You never mentioned any of this to me. We were still seeing each other at that time."

"Of course, I didn't. I didn't tell anyone. His parents would have had a fit if they knew. I tried to talk him out of it, but he was earning so much money and getting a lot of attention from these fans. There was no way he was going to quit. So, I advised him on the practical side of things — the best way to film, the kind of cameras and lighting equipment he should use. He listened, too, and bought the best. He could afford it. I went to his flat once, and he had converted one of the bedrooms into a mini studio. Some of his equipment was even better than mine."

Harry nudged him, getting impatient. "What's this got to do with Tom?" He wasn't sure he was going to like the answer.

"I'll get to that. So, Niko mainly posted straight content to begin with. Videos of him having sex with girls, but he had a lot of gay followers. He was a good-looking young man and very popular. He started tailoring his posts to that audience — a lot of naked photos of himself — jerk-off videos, you know the kind of thing. And of course, his subscriptions went through the roof. He had a whole new set of fans who expected more and more from him."

Harry swallowed. He had a good idea where this was going now. "You mean he was gay for pay? I think a lot of models do that. They make more money, right?"

Antoni nodded. "The solo jerk-off videos progressed to him jerking off with other guys."

The weight inside Harry grew heavier. "Are you telling me Tom was one of those guys?"

Antoni side-eyed him and nodded. "If what Niko told me was true, there were quite a lot of men involved. The subscribers expect regular updates and fresh content. Tom did a couple of videos with Niko. Reece Wallace, too. Some men from Newcastle. They're just the ones I know about."

"But why? Tom loved Sarah."

"Money, I guess. It wasn't really about sex. Niko saw it as a business. Tom probably earned more in an hour with Niko than a whole day on the boat with you."

"Okay, but this still doesn't make sense. Why would someone kill them for a few harmless videos? It's not like anyone close to him even knew about them."

"I don't know that they did. Maybe it had nothing to do with the videos, but it's a secret that connects two of the victims. Maybe the third man was involved, too. I don't know everything. That's why I have to tell the police, so they can look into it."

Harry shook his head. Tom's family had enough to cope with. If what Antoni was saying was true, they would be devastated further. "Oh, shit. This is... You're going to the police?"

"I must. I'll tell them everything I know, and maybe they can fill in some of the gaps. There's probably a lot more to it than even I'm aware of."

Harry nodded slowly. "You didn't think about coming forward sooner?"

"I've already told you that. I wasn't sure how relevant it was at first. And if it wasn't, it would hurt so many people. It was only later, after Tom... God, I regret it so much already. If I'd spoken sooner, Tom might still be alive."

Harry didn't know what else to say. While he couldn't blame Antoni for Tom's death, if he hadn't waited a week to come forward with what he knew, it would have been avoided. "Okay, you need to speak to the police now, before anyone else gets hurt." He pulled out his phone. It had gone five o'clock. "Let's head back to the gallery and you can call them from there."

He noticed he had a text message and opened it. It was from Christian.

"Shit," he said. "The police are already looking for Reece Wallace." He showed Antoni the phone.

Antoni's eyes widened. "Reece? No. It can't be him."

"Didn't you just say he was one of Niko's models?"

"Yes, but…"

"Come on. Let's go. The sooner you tell the police what you know, the better."

* * * *

Christian couldn't sit still. Dominic and Arnie did their best to calm him, but all he could think about was Harry. After twenty minutes or so, Harry replied to his text message.

I can't believe it. I'm on South Pier with Antoni but going back to town now. Antoni has info for the police.

Christian jumped to his feet and hurried to collect his coat. "If he's with Antoni, they're probably heading to the gallery. I'll meet them there."

"I'll drive you," Dominic offered.

"No. It'll be quicker to walk." There was no direct route by road. Dominic would have to navigate the tight back streets. It would be more direct for him to head down from North Point and through the harbour.

"Text us when you get there," Arnie said, "so we know you are all right."

Christian agreed and hurried out of the door. He was probably overreacting, but years of experience as a journalist had taught him to trust his instincts. He needed to be with Harry. There had been enough disasters already. He wouldn't risk another one.

The force of the wind took him by surprise when he left the house. North Point was the highest peak in Nyemouth and the gale cut straight across it with little shelter. Christian tucked his chin in and hurried down the bank.

He wondered what Harry had meant in his text. Antoni has information. *About what? Reece Wallace?* Whatever it was, the sooner he shared it with the police, the sooner it would be over. The situation had gone far enough.

Christian knew nothing about Reece other than what little Harry had told him. He'd helped on the boat earlier in the week when Tom had taken ill. He wondered how much Harry trusted the young man. If he encountered Reece before the police made an arrest, would he try to reason with him? Christian hoped not. It would be better to keep well away until they knew exactly why he was wanted.

In all his years on the job, he had never been this personally invested in a story. Like Marie Baxter-Booth, he was used to turning up, following the facts and moving on when it was over. This was different. He couldn't bear the thought of anything happening to Harry now, not when his feelings were so strong. He couldn't keep his mind from running through all the things that could go wrong. Once he had pictured the thought of Harry, fatally wounded, he couldn't turn it off.

Reaching the steep steps down to the harbour, he gripped the railing as the wind buffered him from behind. Despite the dangers, he quickened his pace. The sooner he reached Harry, the easier he would feel.

* * * *

"I don't believe Reece is the kind of man who would do something like this, something so violent," Antoni said.

"Until today, neither did I," Harry remarked. "But it seems people are capable of all kinds of things I couldn't imagine."

They had reached the exit of South Pier and the steep bank leading back to the town centre. The wind howled stronger than ever. There was no point in trying to make a phone call until they had reached a more sheltered area.

"Do you know for certain he's one of the boys in Niko's videos?" Harry asked. "Like, when did he even turn eighteen? Surely he's not old enough."

"He'll be old enough," Antoni answered. "I got the impression from Niko that everything he did was above board and legal. He took it very seriously. He won't have taken the chance of doing anything that might get him banned from the sites. There was too much money at stake. But no, I don't know for sure, only what Niko told me. I haven't seen any of his videos."

"You'll have to tell the police everything."

"I know," Antoni snapped. "And I will. They probably know most of it by now, anyway. Why else would they be looking for him?"

Harry bit his lip. There was no point starting an argument with Antoni. It was a squabble for another time. He had no idea how he was going to explain any of this to Rachel and Tom's family. They were still coming to terms with his death. He couldn't imagine how they would cope learning about his side-line with Niko.

The sky above was black with ominous clouds. It wouldn't get dark for another hour, but the rain looked like it would come away at any second.

Up ahead, he saw a figure in a black waterproof jacket walking down the bank towards them.

Who the hell wants to come out in conditions like this?

As the figure grew closer, he made out their features. "Oh, shit."

"What?" Antoni looked up, catching sight of the man for the first time.

"It's Stew Wallace, Reece's dad. He must be trying to find him before the police do."

Harry couldn't recall when he'd last seen Stew without his flat cap on. He wore it everywhere, even in the pub, but conditions were too wild for a hat today. Stew's thinning, grey hair was whipped back from his face. There had always been a dourness about Stew. Harry had heard him use racist and sexist language about the harbour. He'd also heard rumours that his wife was terrified of him and would often sport bruises on her arms and legs. As far as he could recall, he'd never heard Stew make any homophobic comments, but it would not surprise him. Stew was not the kind of bloke who would take the idea of his son starring in gay-for-pay videos lightly.

Harry raised his hand in an awkward greeting as they came level. "Stew, there's no one out there," he gestured behind them to the pier. "It's getting worse. If you're looking for Reece, he hasn't gone that way."

The fisherman did not seem to hear him. His gaze was fixed straight on Antoni, the anger was evident in his expression and movement.

Oh, shit. He's heard about the videos. He blames Antoni.

Stew marched straight up to Antoni and put one hand on his shoulder. Harry was aware of a sudden, jerking motion of his other arm. A violent jolt as his elbow moved back and forth. Harry knew what had happened before he saw for sure. Antoni tumbled forward, clutching his abdomen.

Stew straightened. The long, narrow knife he used to gut and fillet fish dripped with Antoni's blood.

In a fraction of a second, everything snapped into focus. The police were searching for Reece Wallace, but it was his father they really wanted. Bigoted Stew Wallace was responsible for the murders.

Antoni rolled onto this back. Stew stepped straight over him, coming straight at Harry with the knife.

Harry turned and ran headlong into the wind, back onto the pier.

Chapter Twenty-Two

Christian battled against the elements on South Bank. The wind drove straight into his face, and by the time he had crossed the river, a cold rain had started to fall. It was an abysmal evening. With his head down, he powered across the cobbles, which were now treacherous and slippery. The streets were deserted, though he noticed that several of the bars were full of people taking shelter from the storm.

He kept his phone in his hand the whole way, checking every few minutes to see if there were any more messages from Harry. There had been nothing since his text about being on the pier. Christian headed towards the gallery, hoping that was where Harry and Antoni were making for.

His nerves were still jangling. The brisk pace of his walk didn't help, but he would not relax until he knew Harry was safe. The malignant feeling that the killer would target Harry would not leave. Christian knew he was probably overreacting, but he couldn't silence the fear. Three men were dead already. He couldn't let Harry become the fourth victim.

It had also made him appreciate just how strong his feelings were. They had known each other for less than a week, but the connection they had formed was powerful. Christian couldn't deal with the thought of something happening to Harry now.

He was out of breath when he reached the door of the Northumberland Art Gallery. The lights were on in the window display, but the shop beyond was dark. Christian knocked on the door. Maybe they were out the back somewhere. There had to be more to the premises than the public spaces he had seen. He pressed his face to the glass, shielding his eyes to see further back. When there was no reply, he knocked again, harder this time.

No one came.

The sign on the door said the gallery closed at five on Sunday.

He tried Harry's number. After six rings, it went straight to voicemail.

Shit.

He left a message anyway. "Hey, it's me. I'm outside the gallery now, but there's no answer. If you guys are there, can you let me in?"

He hung up and waited for a call back.

None came.

He wondered if they might have gone directly to the police station. It was located in one of the back streets on the north side of the river. *Surely not.* Harry would have had to pass him. He couldn't have got all the way from the pier to the bridge in the time it had taken Christian to rush down from Dominic's place.

So, where is he? Still at the pier?

It seemed unlikely. It wasn't that far from here — a ten-minute walk at most.

Then the creeping dread intensified. Had Reece Wallace caught up with Harry and Antoni before they made it back? No. It couldn't be. Arnie had to be right about Reece fleeing Nyemouth. Why wouldn't he when the police were looking to arrest him?

Because he's a killer. Because he's not in the right frame of mind.

Fuck it. Christian couldn't wait around doing nothing. It would be dark soon. He had to find Harry and make sure he was safe.

His feet slipped as he sprinted along Pier Street. Christian caught himself and kept from falling over. Undeterred, he pressed on.

* * * *

Stew Wallace had a large, lumbering frame and Harry outran him easily, however he realised in an instant what a mistake he had made heading onto the pier. He was trapped. It had been the only option. To the right, the cliff face was sheer and insurmountable. If he'd gone left, he would never have made it across the jagged rocks to the safety of the seafront cottages. The waves were already washing over them.

And what of Antoni?

He risked a look behind. Stew was still coming, a good twenty feet behind him — and beyond, Antoni was on the ground, clutching his stomach. Harry saw movement. He was alive. Badly wounded, but not out. Now Harry had to save himself if Antoni was to stand a chance.

Stew had the knife and came at him in a demented rage.

What the hell has gotten into him?

Is he really crazy enough to kill because his son shot a few raunchy video clips?

The answer was obviously yes.

A colossal wave hit the pier sideways on. Harry ducked as it sprayed its spume forty feet above his head. It pulled him to the right as it washed over the boards. He steadied himself before getting up and running again. It was far too dangerous to be out here, even without the crazed knife-carrying man.

Harry darted towards the lighthouse. The wooden boards were slippery underfoot, but he had to keep going. Even as he ran, he knew it was hopeless. The lighthouse was automated, and the doors were bound to be locked, but it was his only chance. If he could get inside and shut Stew out, he'd have a chance of raising the alarm.

Another wave hit, even bigger than the first. Harry leapt sideways, throwing his body against the railings, gripping them tight as the backwash poured down on him, threatening to take him over. The force of the water was like nothing he'd ever known. He held on until it had passed.

He looked back in the hope it might have taken Stew—or even just his knife. No such luck. The fisherman was on his feet again, closing the gap between them.

In a daze, Harry started for the lighthouse once more.

At its base, three stone steps led to the door. He bolted, ascended them three at a time, and clutched the handle. Locked. *Damn it.* He rattled, knowing it was hopeless. There was no one inside.

Focus on survival.

He turned in time to see that Stew was almost upon him. The thin knife arched through the air.

Harry had no self-defence training. Having spent the whole of his life in this small town, working on and around boats, he had never needed it. Now he cursed that mistake. As Stew came at him, the knife intent on its target, Harry reacted on instinct without thought or planning. He dropped, sliding down the three stone steps, ducking out of Stew's reach.

The fisherman snorted frustration, turning upon him.

Harry kicked, going straight for his shins, putting as much force as he possessed into the thrust. Stew snarled, falling backwards, losing his balance just as another wave struck the pier.

For several seconds, Harry couldn't see a thing. The saltwater that surged over him stung his eyes. He dug his fingers into the space between the boards, gripping against the force of the wash back. When he opened his eyes again, Stew had been carried six feet towards the railing.

The fisherman rose to his knees, shaking off the spray.

He still had the knife.

Will this nightmare ever end?

* * * *

Christian reached the top of the bank that led to the pier. In the darkening gloom, it took his mind a moment to understand what he was seeing. To the seaward side, the grey waves were mountainous, smashing to shore and sending great columns of spray into the air, dwarfing the wooden structure.

Then he spotted someone on the ground, near the bottom of the ramp. Christian rushed forward. The figure wore a red coat. He was certain he hadn't seen Harry dressed in anything like it, but it didn't ease his anxiety. As he got closer, he saw that the man on the ground was hurt.

It was Antoni.

"Oh, my God. What happened?" Christian crouched beside him. Antoni clutched his side, covering the stain of darker red that spread across the jacket. There was a pool of blood beneath him, running away with the rain down the bank.

"I've been stabbed," Antoni gasped. "Stew Wallace. He's got a knife."

Christian raised his phone and hit the fast dial for an emergency. When the operator answered, the line was as bad as his earlier call to Harry.

"I don't know if you can hear me," he spoke slowly, his voice possessed by a calmness he did not feel. "I'm at the south pier in Nyemouth. There's a man here with a serious stomach wound. He's been stabbed and is losing blood. He needs an ambulance, fast."

Antoni gripped his wrist. "Stew," he croaked. "He's gone after Harry. On the pier... Stop him."

Christian's blood ran even colder. "Police, too," he barked into the phone. "Stew Wallace is the man you want. He's here. *Get here now.*" He handed the phone to Antoni. "Keep talking. Tell them everything you can. I don't know how much they can even hear, but just keep trying."

Antoni nodded.

"Will you be okay?" He was torn. Antoni needed his help, but he was still alive. Right now, he didn't know where Harry was or what condition he was in.

"Go on," Antoni urged. "*Now*."

Christian left him, sprinting to the pier.

Smaller swells battered the lower structure, but every third or fifth wave was a monster that came completely over the top. Christian squinted, trying to see clearly.

There.

Two figures out towards the end, close to the lighthouse.

As he ran onto the wet boards, he was shocked at how unsteady they were. The force of the sea and the wind caused them to shudder beneath his feet. His sneakers gained a poor purchase as he tried to race ahead, ducking each time one of the giant waves came over.

He lost his footing beneath the strength of one downpour and was carried towards the edge. In a panic, he thrashed in all directions, desperately reaching for a hold.

Shit. This is it. This is the end.

Just before it seemed like he was going, he rolled onto his stomach and flattened his body against the wood. He curled his fingers around two boards, dug in with his feet and knees and held on until the worst had passed.

Trembling, he rose unsteadily to his feet.

Harry.

Desperation to save the man he loved propelled him forward.

Neither Harry nor Stew were aware of his approach. The storm granted him that small favour, covering all sounds of his progress. He had to use that surprise to his advantage. It might be the only thing he had.

Stew Wallace bore down on Harry, a viscous-looking knife in his hand. Christian had seen the damage that blade had done to Antoni. The man was crazed. He had stabbed four men so far this week, three of them fatally. Christian wouldn't let him add to that tally.

He rushed forward, crouching low, and hit him with a rugby tackle, shoving his shoulder against Stew's thighs and knocking him sideways. They both hit the deck.

Stew struggled, getting his knee into Christian's chin. He tasted blood but held on as Stew shuffled away from him. His clothes were soaked, and Christian lost his grip. Stew stumbled ahead and made it to his knees again. He turned on Christian in a flash, the blade streaking through the air.

Christian raised an arm to protect himself and the knife slashed downwards on his forearm. He felt the scrape of steel against bone before the pain hit. Stew had some momentum now, and as Christian rolled onto his back, the heavier man used his weight to pin him down.

Stew was demented, his lips drawn back from his teeth in an expression of pure savagery. Christian understood in that second what Stew was capable of. He had killed those other boys and would kill Harry and him right now if they didn't fight back.

They were taken suddenly by the crash of another huge wave. The force of it washing over them pressed Stew down harder against him. Christian pushed back as the pressure subsided and tried to scramble backwards, away from the madman.

Then he saw another sudden flash of steel above his belly.

The blade slid effortlessly into his flesh. Christian stared in disbelief.

He's actually stabbed me.

Within seconds, he was blinded by the intensity of sickening pain.

Chapter Twenty-Three

For a brief moment, time seemed to run slowly. Harry watched as Stew stuck the knife into Christian, but he was powerless to stop him. It happened so fast. Harry screamed in despair as the blade disappeared to the hilt. The sound seemed to break the spell Stew was under. He looked from Christian to Harry and back again, as though only just realising they were two different people.

I have to get him away from Christian. It's his only chance.

Harry tried to think rationally. He had three options. Lead him back to shore, get the knife or lure him close enough to the edge that he could push him over with the next freak wave. The third option was the most dangerous. If it worked, there was a high chance that he would fall with Stew.

Stew rose to his feet, his attention fixed on Harry. That meant Christian was safe, for now at least.

"What the hell is this about?" Harry said. "Come on, Stew. You've known me all my life. You can stop now. Don't make it any worse than it already is."

Stew hesitated. The first hint of uncertainty crossed his face.

Harry thought about running. Stew's confusion could give him the head start he needed. Could he outrun him all the way back to town? At any other time, the answer would have been yes but not in this storm. Harry would only have to slip once to give Stew an advantage. And if he stuck that thing into Harry, there would be no hope for Christian and Antoni afterwards.

"Come on, Stew. It's me, Harry. Jack Renner's son. You know who I am. I'm not going to hurt you. I'm your friend, remember?"

Harry combed his expression for any hint that his words were getting through to him.

"You taught me how to shell prawns when I was just a kid. Remember? We'd sit on the deck of your boat with a huge bucket of them, working our way through. You showed me how to do it without damaging the flesh inside. Remember that?"

Stew's eyes widened. The knife hand lowered a fraction.

"Stew," Harry implored, "please. Just throw that thing away and we can head back. Get dried off and warm, huh? Think about Reece — about how he'll feel when he hears about this."

"Reece?" Stew seemed lost. For a second, his focus was entirely inwards, then he snapped back to the present, and his expression was pure white fury. "*You.* You did this to my boy. Baited him to make that filth. You ruined him."

Stew ran towards him.

Get the knife. It was the only safe option now.

Stew came in low, the blade angled towards Harry's midsection — the same place the fucker had stabbed all those other men. Harry bided his time, letting Stew get close before ducking to the side. Stew's weight worked against him, and he flew past, skidding, going to his knees. He tumbled face forward.

Harry pressed home his advantage. Whatever happened now, he was not about to run away. He would go down fighting.

He threw himself across Stew's back. He didn't have the size benefit of the older man but pushed him down with all he had, going for the knife. Stew held the blade beyond his reach, struggling beneath him. Harry realised he was in danger of being toppled off if he didn't do something else...and fast.

He grabbed Stew's head in both hands, pulling it backwards before slamming it against the boards with all his strength. Despite the howl of wind and crash of waves beneath them, Harry heard the crack of Stew's nose, followed by a roar of pain. Without thinking, Harry repeated the action, banging his head against the pier.

Stew let go of the knife.

Harry scrambled over him, focused solely on grabbing the weapon and getting rid of it. Without it, he was confident he could take the older man in a fist fight, should it come to that.

Stew reared upwards, toppling Harry from his back. Harry fell sideways.

The knife.

He crawled forward and got his fingers around the handle, but Stew shouldered him aside. Despite the injury, the older man remained agile. Harry put on a renewed burst of speed. He briefly touched the handle again before Stew crashed against him with a roar of rage. Stew's balled fist flew into Harry's belly. The thickness of his coat took most of the impact. Undeterred, Harry went for the blade again.

The knife was less than a centimetre from a gap in the wooden boards. Harry had no intention of picking it up now. All that mattered was getting rid of it. He kicked Stew, getting a good blow to his chest. Suddenly free of his grip, Harry spurted forward. His fingertips touched the knife handle. Just one push was all it took.

The knife slid between the gap in the boards and fell into the sea below.

The loss of the weapon seemed to rekindle Stew's rage.

He was on top of Harry again, covering his back. The older man laid into Harry with his fists, pounding into the soft tissue of his lower torso, aiming for the kidneys and liver. Pain exploded inside him, but he wasn't about to give in yet.

They were drenched by the force of a fresh wave. The cold water brought the weight of Stew's body down even heavier on him. Harry found it difficult to breathe. He managed to free an arm from underneath and smashed it backwards, striking Stew's face with luck rather than skilled aim. Stew howled and relaxed his grip enough for Harry to shuffle free.

Then, above the sound of the wind and sea, he heard something else. *Sirens.*

Dragging his body away from Stew, Harry looked up to see the flash of blue lights at the top of the bank. The police were on their way.

There was no time to relax yet.

He rolled over and rose to a sitting position. He was close to the railing and gripped it for support.

Stew was on his knees a couple of yards away. He held his hand to his lower face. Blood poured over his knuckles and some of the fight had left him.

"It's over," Harry shouted. "Can't you hear it? The police are coming. Give yourself up, for the sake of your family. Do you have any idea what this will do to them?"

Stew got his balance back and rose to his feet, still clutching his bloody nose. He gazed in the direction of the sirens. Two police cars and an ambulance were at the top of the bank. Uniformed figures raced along the path.

"It's finished," Harry shouted. "Give up."

Stew didn't even look at him. With his eyes fixed on the flashing lights, he stumbled to the railing on the opposite side of the pier. Harry realised what he was about to do but didn't have the energy left to stop him. Stew climbed onto the rail.

Harry bowed his head as the next wave washed over the top. When the water drained away and he opened his eyes, Stew Wallace was gone.

Christian.

Harry crawled on all fours towards him. Christian lay on his side, curled in a foetal position, not moving.

"Christian," he called, climbing over him.

Christian held his hands folded across his abdomen. There was a cut on his arm which didn't look serious. It was the belly wound that concerned Harry the most. He shook Christian's shoulder. He was freezing to the touch.

His eyes fluttered.

Thank God.

Harry looked along the pier. The police and ambulance were parked up, but there was no sign of them coming out to get them. *Shit. Do they even know we're here?*

Depending on what Antoni was able to tell them, they might not.

"Hey," Harry hollered, "over here."

Useless. His words were taken in the wrong direction by the wind.

He gave Christian another shake and his eyes opened wide.

"I'm sorry, darling, but I'm going to have to move you. We need to get to the shore. I don't think they know we're here."

"Stew?" Christian croaked.

"Don't worry. He's gone."

"Did…did he hurt you?"

"Nothing serious. A few bruises. Don't worry about me."

Christian gasped and grimaced as Harry eased him into a sitting position. "Fuck. The bastard got me good."

"He won't be getting anyone else," Harry said. He moved into a squat position and wrapped Christian's good arm around his shoulder. "Put all of your weight on me and see if you can get up."

As soon as he tried to stand, Christian cried in pain. Harry eased him back as another wave came over. Harry protected him as best he could, taking most of the force.

"You go," Christian gasped. "I can't make it. You go back and send help."

"No fucking way. After all that we've been through, I'm not leaving you." He shuffled around, getting both hands beneath Christian's shoulders and holding him in the sitting position. "I'm going to drag you along, okay? It's going to be rough, but try to hold out as long as you can, all right? I'll stop if you need me to, but the sooner we get this done, the better."

Christian nodded.

With his waterlogged clothes, he was heavier than Harry imagined, but drawing on an unknown reserve of strength, Harry lifted him enough to drag him backwards with just his heels trailing on the boards. He heaved and fought against the pain in his own back, making pitiful progress, pausing whenever they were beset by waves.

Halfway there, Christian stopped groaning. Harry prayed he had only passed out with the pain and nothing more serious. The urgency made him redouble his effort, making progress one agonising foot at a time.

Then there were voices behind him. He glanced over his shoulder and saw police and paramedics running in their direction.

With a cry, he lowered Christian to the boards, supporting his head and shoulders against his thighs. "It's all right," he said, stroking his brow. "Help is here. It's over."

"Where's Stew Wallace?" one of the police officers shouted.

"He's gone…into the sea."

"Is there anyone else out there? Is anybody hurt?"

"Just Christian. He's been stabbed in the stomach and the arm. Help him. Won't you please do something?"

The paramedics reached them, going straight to work, assessing Christian's wounds.

"It's all right," a voice said. "We've got you now. You're both safe."

Chapter Twenty-Four

Harry spent the night in the hospital being treated for hypothermia, shock and a broken rib. Despite the best intentions of the medical staff, he didn't care about his own condition. All that mattered was knowing that Christian was okay. The doctor, an exhausted looking woman in her mid-twenties, informed him that Christian was in surgery and they would update him as soon as they had news.

"We need to get in touch with Mr. Coster's next of kin," a nurse in his forties later enquired. "Do you have any contact details?"

Next of kin. Harry panicked. "Does that mean he didn't make it?"

The nurse's expression was reassuring. "He's stable. He's in recovery now. But we need to let his family, if he has any, know what has happened."

Relief flooded his body. All the tension he'd been holding faded away. "He didn't say too much. We've only known each other a week. His parents retired to Norway, but he has a brother and sister in this country.

He works for the *Manchester Gazette*. Contact them and they will have his personal details on file."

"I'll give them a call."

"Can you let me know as soon as you know more about how he is doing?"

The nurse smiled and adjusted Harry's oxygen mask, making it secure. "I will. In the meantime, try to relax and sleep a little. You've had a tough time of it yourself."

Sleep did not seem possible, but eventually his brain gave in, and he fell into a deep, exhausted slumber.

* * * *

When Harry woke up the next morning, the ward was coming to life. Nurses and care assistants moved around the beds, carrying out their morning checks and delivering medication. The bed next to him that had been empty when he arrived was occupied. Harry rose into a sitting position so he could see.

Christian.

He was asleep on his back. His breath was deep but sound. He was hooked up to some machinery that Harry didn't understand, but no alarms were ringing, and everything looked okay. They had erected a frame beneath the covers to keep the bedclothes off his midsection, and his right arm was bandaged from wrist to elbow.

Harry wiped his eyes. Christian looked so frail and vulnerable.

But alive, he told himself. *The most important thing is that he's alive.*

When the consultant came along on his morning rounds and checked Harry over, he was discharged with painkillers for the broken rib. His parents arrived with clean clothes.

"I want to stay a while," he told them, once he had dressed. "Just until he wakes up. I don't want him to be alone."

They understood and left him in the chair beside Christian's bed. The nurses informed him they'd made contact with Christian's brother, and he would arrive later that morning.

Not long after ten, Christian opened his eyes. He blinked and looked around in confusion before he saw Harry.

Harry took his good hand. "Hey. Welcome back. How do you feel?"

"Sore as hell." But there was relief in his voice. "Did they fix me up?"

Harry nodded. "You'll have a few more scars to show for it, but you'll survive."

Christian slowly licked his lips. "My mouth is dry."

Harry poured him a glass of water and held it to his lips. "Just sips, okay. Take your time. It's probably an after-effect of the anaesthetic."

Christian did as he asked and swallowed carefully. "Stew? What happened to him?"

"Missing, presumed dead. According to my dad, the lifeboat is still searching this morning, but there is no expectation that they'll find him alive—not after so long in the water."

"Did he hurt you?"

"He got a few kicks in. Nothing to worry about. When the police arrived, he jumped into the sea rather than let them take him. You saw the conditions last night. There's no chance that he survived."

"Shit." Christian exhaled and starved at the ceiling. After a while, he looked back at Harry and asked, "Why did he do it? Does anyone know?"

"They are still putting the pieces together. I think he just lost it." He told Christian what he'd learned from Antoni—about Niko's online sex business and the scenes he'd filmed with Tom and Reece.

"He killed three men because his son shot a few jerk-off videos with other guys?" Christian sounded incredulous. "What about the second victim? Ike. Was he also in the videos?"

"Nobody really knows. The investigation is ongoing. According to my parents, the police are talking to Reece right now. Maybe he'll be able to fill in some of the gaps. Stew has always been a strange one. He was always there, wanting to revel in gossip and other people's misfortunes, but he didn't like it when attention was turned the other way. He kept his own life very private. His wife, Beverley, barely went out. He never took her to the club, or for a meal. I suspect he was extremely controlling—misogynistic, racist, homophobic. He must have lost it when he learned what Reece had been up to."

"Bastard." Christian's voice was little more than a whisper. "He murdered three men and was prepared to kill you, Antoni and anyone else who might know about it."

"Whatever his reasons were in the beginning, I suspect he'd lost all rationale by yesterday. He was crazy when he came for me. And to chuck himself in the sea rather than be caught? Something inside him had snapped."

Christian entwined his fingers with Harry's. "You fought him off, though. You were a hero."

He had to stop himself from laughing. It hurt too much. "I wouldn't say that. I did what I had to do for all of us to survive."

"What about Antoni?" Christian asked, jerking upwards in bed and then lowering back down in obvious pain. "Is he okay?"

"They've got him on another ward. I haven't seen him yet, but the nurse told me he'll pull through, too. He had surgery just like you did. I'm starting to feel left out. The pair of you will have your battle scars and I've got a broken rib, which will heal with no obvious signs."

Christian gripped his hand even tighter. "You'll be scarred by this experience in other ways — and sometimes the ones that don't show are the worst."

* * * *

Antoni's brother, Roger, came onto the ward later in the morning. There were black shadows beneath his eyes. He looked like he hadn't slept all night. Harry rose to hug him, careful to keep his injured side turned away.

"How is he?" Harry asked.

"Doing okay?" Roger replied. "He asked me to check on you both before I go home. They have performed some kind of surgery on his abdomen, but the doctor says he's been very lucky. If Wallace had used a thicker knife or stabbed him half an inch higher, it would have been a far worse situation."

Harry gasped. "Shit. I still can't get my head around this."

"I'm glad your brother will be okay," Christian said. "Let him know we are worried about him, too."

Roger gave a grim-faced nod. "I think he's taking it badly. He is blaming himself for all of it."

"No," Harry said firmly. "Tell him that's bullshit. In fact, don't tell him. When Christian's brother arrives, I'll go up and put him straight myself. There is only one person responsible for any of this, and it's Stew."

"Harry is right," Christian said. "I don't think Antoni could have done anything to stop him. He was set on his path. If the police had pulled his son in for questioning earlier in the week, it would likely just have triggered his final assault sooner."

Roger's shoulders visibly sagged. "I think you're right, but Antoni will take some convincing."

"Then we are the people to do it. Don't worry. We won't let him carry this alone," Harry said.

"I spoke to the mother of the second victim, Ike Meeker," Christian said. "She came in during the night, looking for news. The staff wouldn't let her near any of you guys, but I saw her in the canteen while I waited for my brother to come out of surgery. I told her as much as the police had told me at the time, which was not a lot. She confirmed that the police believe Stew Wallace is responsible for Ike's death, too."

"Bastard," Christian cursed.

"Any idea why? Was he involved in the videos, too?" Harry asked.

"Ike was Niko's photographer and editor. He filmed the videos and put them together. For all he worked in a supermarket, he had a degree in media studies. Like Niko, the online business was a side-line."

"And his laptop and phone were stolen? Right?" Christian asked.

Roger nodded again.

"Shit!" Harry gasped. He sat back down. "But I still don't get why he came after me and Antoni. Why not go after the other boys who Niko worked with?"

Roger shook his head. "I have no idea."

"He probably didn't know who they were or where to find them," Christian said. "Models don't use their real names online, and unless he was clever enough to hack Niko's personal records, which seems unlikely, he'd have no way of tracking them down. I think he was targeting the people he did know. His son must have told him about Antoni giving Niko advice about how to film and all the technical stuff. And he probably thought you were involved, or at least knew about it, because of Tom. He wasn't thinking rationally. Certainly not by last night, he wasn't."

Harry signed again and shook his head. "I guess we'll never really know, not now that the bastard is gone."

"Yeah," said Christian. "And good-fucking-riddance."

Chapter Twenty-Five

Three months later

Christian arrived in Nyemouth late on Friday evening. The traffic out of Manchester had been the usual nightmare and little better on the M62 and A1. The journey had seemed like it would never end.

It had been a long week since he'd last seen Harry on Monday morning. They were taking it in turn to travel to each other on alternate weekends. It wasn't ideal, but they had managed to make it work so far. He knew that wouldn't last. Come the summer, Harry would have little free time to travel across the country to see him.

Other couples made it work over greater distances, but they were not like other couples. Christian didn't want to spend so much time apart from the man he loved.

There were no parking spaces in front of Harry's flat. He drove around to the alley behind and pulled in. It was dark and cold when he stepped out of the car. He grabbed his overcoat from the boot, along with his weekend bag, and opened the gate to the rear of the property.

The lights were on in the kitchen.

His heart leapt when he saw Harry through the window, looking gorgeous in a simple black T-shirt. Christian locked the gate behind him and hurried to the back door. He could barely contain his anticipation as he knocked.

Harry unlocked the door and welcomed him with a broad smile and open arms.

"Hello, sexy," he said.

"I've missed you," Christian said, stepping into his embrace and hugging him tight.

They kissed, long and deep, and Christian savoured every second.

"Sorry I'm so late. I wanted to get away early, but something came up. Then the bloody traffic was a nightmare."

"You're here now," Harry said, hugging him tighter. Christian always followed Harry's lead when they embraced now, frightened of hurting him. Harry insisted his broken rib had healed, but Christian had caught the way he grimaced sometimes when he thought no one was looking.

"Something smells good," he said, following Harry into the kitchen.

"I'm just sweating some shallots and garlic down. I've got some fresh mussels, all prepped and ready to go." Harry went to the stove and turned off the heat. "You're not hungry just yet, are you?"

"Only for you," he quipped.

Harry raised his brows mischievously. "You might have to wait a little bit longer for that, too. Put your coat on. You'll need it." Harry pulled a dark sweater over his T-shirt and fetched his heavy jacket from the cupboard.

"What is this?" Christian asked, putting on his coat.

"A surprise," Harry said, barely hiding his excitement.

Christian chuckled and patted his pert bottom as he followed him to the front door. As they stepped outside, he suddenly realised what this was about.

"It's arrived?"

Harry grinned. "Collected her yesterday. Dad and I went down to Whitby and brought her back."

"Oh, my God. Congratulations. Come on then. Don't hang about. Show me."

Laughing, they walked down to the harbour.

The new boat was berthed in the place he used to keep the old vessel.

Harry had been adamant last autumn that he would never set foot on *The North Star* again, not after what had happened to Tom and Niko. Though he loved the boat, it held too many bad memories. He'd sold it to a tour company in the Farne Islands. They intended to refit and rename *The North Star* and use it to run seal-watching trips. Christian had expected Harry to be devastated when the boat had been taken away in December, but he had shown no emotion when the new owners steered her out of the harbour.

"Wow," he exclaimed, looking down from the dock at the new vessel. "This looks a lot bigger."

"Not massively so, but longer and a little wider. There's more cabin space, too. She's about twenty years younger than *The North Star*, so she should be more efficient and stable."

"Looks beautiful. Can we go on deck?"

Harry nodded. "Let me get the lights first. It's dark down there. I don't want you slipping."

Harry scooted down the ladder and crossed the deck to the wheelhouse. He unlocked the cabin door and turned on the lights, illuminating the whole boat.

Now Christian could see just how different this was to the old vessel. Everything from the deck to the fixtures and fittings looked new. He sat on the edge of the dock, swung his legs over and climbed down the ladder. Harry was waiting at the bottom to help him aboard.

"She's beautiful. I'm so pleased for you." Christian put his arm over Harry's shoulder.

"She's recently been refurbished, so there's not a lot for me to do. Just a change of name and she'll be ready to go."

"What will you call her?"

"*Absent Friends*."

Emotion welled and caught in Christian's throat. "That's lovely."

"Come into the cabin."

It was much larger than the old boat. The wheel and technical equipment were on a consul at the front, while to the left there was a bank of fixed seats, to the right a table and more seats.

"This is perfect. You'll be so happy onboard her."

"Sit. I've got something to help us celebrate." Harry disappeared down a set of stairs to a lower deck.

Christian made himself comfortable at the table. There was a real sense of newness about the interior. The previous owners must have carried out their refit very recently. It was a stroke of luck that it had come on the market just as Harry was looking. After all the things he'd had to endure, Harry deserved some good fortune.

Harry came back up the steps with a bottle of champagne and a plate of food. "Langoustines," he declared. "Fresh today. I cooked them a little while ago. Can you open the bottle while I get the glasses?" He hurried below deck again.

Christian had the bottle uncorked for his return and filled the champagne flutes.

"Cheers," he said, clinking glasses with Harry. "To every success onboard your new boat."

"And to all our absent friends," Harry added.

"Absolutely."

The champagne was perfect. The food equally so.

As Christian looked across the table, he couldn't remember ever feeling this happy. The future seemed full of endless hope and possibilities.

"Seeing as we're celebrating, how would you feel if I shared some news, too?" He took another sip.

Harry's eyes shone like amber in the low light of the cabin. "I'm all ears."

Christian took a breath. "Well, I had an interview for a new job this week. It was all done online, so I haven't actually met the team. I didn't want to mention it to you until I was certain, but they called this afternoon and offered me the job."

Harry's brow furrowed. "They did? What is it? Where is it?"

Christian grinned as he dragged it out. "Here."

Harry opened his mouth in delight. "You're kidding?"

"Nope. Well, it's not exactly here in Nyemouth. It's with a paper in Newcastle. But it's a damned sight nearer than Manchester."

"Oh, my God. Are you sure about this? Isn't it a comedown? Career-wise, I mean."

"Yes and no. It depends how you look at it. The salary is a lot less, but then so are the rental prices in Nyemouth compared to my flat in the centre of Manchester. It's also part-time, just four days per week, which means I'll have more time to devote to my novels. And best of all—and I hope you agree on this part—it means we can see each other every day instead of just weekends."

Harry bolted out of his seat and flew around the table. He wrapped his arms around Christian and hugged him, pressing their heads together. "Yes. Yes. Yes. Oh my God, this is the best news. Shit, I can't believe it. I'm so happy."

"I was hoping that would be the reaction. It's been chewing me up all the way here, wondering if this was going too quickly for you."

"After everything we've been through already, I feel like I've known you for years."

Christian struggled for breath. His chest was tight with emotion. "I feel the same. I'm glad you do, too."

Harry straightened and wiped his eyes with the back of his hands. "I hate not seeing you during the week. I know we'd said we'd give the long-distance relationship thing a try, but this is so much better."

"I think so, too," Christian said, taking his hand and pressing a kiss to it.

"And none of this crap about you renting a place. I know my flat is tiny, but it will do for now. You can move straight in. If we eventually find somewhere bigger, I can do the flat up and let it out as summer rental like the floor above. This is a win-win situation. Right?"

Christian smiled and took him in a deeper hug. He didn't know what else to say. It was all so overwhelming.

"Thank you," Harry whispered against his cheek. "Thanks for making me so happy. I don't think I could have survived the last few months without you."

"You would. You're a lot stronger than you think. Remember… You saved my life. And I'm happy I'll get to spend the rest of it with you."

Harry stepped aside and refilled their glasses. "I had no idea we'd have so much to celebrate when I bought this bottle. I should have gotten a whole case."

They raised their glasses to another toast.

"To fresh starts and new beginnings," Christian said.

As they brought the glasses together, he had a good feeling that there would be many more things to celebrate in their future.

Want to see more from this author?
Here's a taster for you to enjoy!

Success: The Runner
Thom Collins

Excerpt

After a few minutes of light-hearted banter with his co-host Lanita, Alex Shaefer brought his weekly podcast to a close. There were never enough hours in the day for Alex to achieve all the things he wanted, and with today's recording running half an hour over, time was getting tight.

"Nice one," Lanita said, reaching across the desk to give him a high-five.

"Is that everything?" Alex asked their producer Naz. "Have we got enough?"

Naz gave a thumbs-up through the studio window. "All good."

Alex let out a long exhalation and took off his headphones.

The Long Run was Alex's baby. The podcast was coming to the end of a second successful year that had seen it move from being an independent broadcast in its first seven months onto the wider platform of the BBC. The original concept had been to focus on British athletics, but they had widened their remit to cover all aspects of sport. Lanita Khan, a well-known football pundit, had joined the team when the show expanded, taking it to even greater triumphs.

With success came more work. The show took longer than ever to put together — booking guests, researching subjects and covering all the latest sports news and gossip. It was a relentless cycle each week. As a sideline, it had almost become a full-time job in itself. At least the move to the BBC had saved him from having to chase the sponsorship and funding deals that had been essential for them as an indie. Because podcasts were free to listen to and so many kids were doing them for fun from their bedrooms, a lot of people were surprised to learn how expensive it was to put a professional-sounding show together and get it on the air.

It was done — for today, at least. Tomorrow the work would start all over on next week's production.

Alex ran his fingers through his dark brown hair, pushing it back from his forehead in thick waves.

"Relax," Lanita said, obviously noticing his tension.

"I can't help it. You know how much I hate having to do the front and centre promotion. That stuff kills me."

Lanita grinned. "Babe, I don't want to sound rude, but you've got nothing to worry about. Sure, you wrote the book, but no one will pay you much attention. You know that, right? All eyes will be on Fernando."

"I hope that's true," he said, unconvinced.

Tonight was the launch of *Playing with Pride*, the official autobiography of Fernando Inglesias. Fernando had made headlines late in the past year when he'd become the first premiership footballer to come out as gay. It was sensational news, which had caused headlines around the world. Everybody had wanted his story. At the time, Alex had dedicated an entire episode of the podcast to the issue of homophobia, not just in football but in sport in general. It was one of his most streamed shows and had resulted in him being asked to speak on several TV programmes.

It had been a huge shock to receive a call three weeks later, asking if he'd like to write Fernando's story for a book. Alex had ghostwritten three other sporting biographies, and the experience had been far from fulfilling. The majority of the subjects for those biographies were people who had no interest in books or even reading, beyond the advance they were offered from the publishers. Sitting down with a writer to flesh out the details of their life and career was often the last thing any of the sporting icons wanted to do. It had been a dismal experience working with those people.

"Things will be different this time." That was what he'd been promised. He'd have unrestricted access to Fernando for the period of research and full credit for having written the book, not just a mention in the acknowledgement section.

Despite his reservations about writing another sports bio, the offer had been too good for him to refuse, and against all expectations, Fernando had come through and acknowledged Alex as his co-writer on *Playing with Pride*. It was a bold step and one which he was grateful for, even when that meant accompanying Fernando on the publicity circuit.

They'd already given joint interviews to several media outlets. *No big deal.* That was part of Alex's business. After completing an MA in sports journalism in his early twenties and gaining his first job at BBC Radio, he'd been in the profession sixteen years and knew how to handle the press.

However, all the other aspects of promotion were a struggle.

To celebrate the book, there would be a huge party in central Manchester. A year after his ground-breaking announcement, Fernando Inglesias was still big news…huge. The pre-sales on *Playing with Pride* were massive. All eyes would be on him, and as his collaborator, Fernando wanted Alex by his side.

"Why don't you tell him you're uncomfortable with this?" Lanita asked.

"I don't want to hurt his feelings. Besides, I've got my name on the cover rather than a ghostwriting credit, so I owe him," Alex said.

"I'm sure he'd understand."

"The trouble is, I think Fernando is nervous too. You know what a big deal this is. He's still the only openly gay player we have. There are plenty of other gay footballers, but no one has followed his lead and come out after him. The guy needs all the support he can get."

She nodded. "And you'll be perfect at it. You always are. Why do *you* get so nervous? You're a natural at what you do."

"Behind the camera," he said. "Radio, podcasting, writing… There's a reason I haven't gone up for any TV presenting jobs. I hate having a camera pointed at me and being the centre of attention."

Lanita rolled her eyes. "You being so unattractive and all."

Alex gave a shy laugh. It wasn't his looks that bothered him about being on camera. He knew he was photogenic, with his strong bone structure and dark hair. Even if he weren't, he didn't care what people thought of him. He just didn't want the attention or adulation that came from appearing on screen or in print—the letters, the emails and IMs that came in the thousands whenever he appeared on TV. There was always a mix of good and bad comments, and they were an unwanted distraction. Alex didn't need any of that to do his job.

As a journalist or reporter, the best asset anyone could have was the ability to walk around unnoticed.

Something inside him clammed up when he was on camera. He could sit in the podcast studio and talk for hours, but the few times he'd been dragged onto TV shows, he'd found himself unable to articulate or express any of the points he needed to make.

He was in a minority. Plenty of other journalists sought fame and attention from TV and social media, and they were welcome to every bit of it.

Alex didn't need or want it.

Lanita gathered her things together, stuffing them inside a huge red leather bag. "C'mon. Let's go. I'm taking you for a drink."

Alex shook his head. "I can't. I have to go home to get ready for the party."

"Bitch, please. What are you going to do? Take a shower and change your shirt? You can do that in fifteen minutes. I know what you're like when you go out, and you don't need two hours to achieve it. C'mon. We're going—me, you and Naz. You know we can't make this evening, and we want to celebrate the book too. I'm buying, so you'd better take advantage of that while you can."

They recorded the podcast at a studio in Media City close to Salford Quays and an array of trendy bars and restaurants. Ten minutes later, they were settled in a comfortable booth with a bottle of champagne on the table.

"To Alex and Fernando," Lanita said, raising a toast.

They clinked glasses.

"When are we gonna get him on the show?" Naz asked. "Fernando, I mean. If anyone can pull a few strings, it's got to be you. We should be all over this book release."

Naz was a good ten years younger than Alex and Lanita but knew more about broadcast technology and recording than the two of them combined. He was a talented kid and had been with the show since the beginning. Alex had picked well when he'd hired him.

"It doesn't feel right, using privilege like that," Alex said. "Besides, there's also the BBC policy about advertising. I can't plug my own book on the show."

"Bullshit," Naz and Lanita said in unison.

"You don't have to mention the book at all," Naz continued. "We just want an interview with Fernando. You know what he would do for our listening figures. Ask him about it tonight."

"No," Alex said firmly. "I'm not going to exploit our friendship for listeners."

"I would," Lanita said. "If I was going to the launch, I wouldn't hesitate. And he would say yes. I'm sure of it."

"How come you're not going?" Naz asked.

"I'm presenting a feature on *The One Show*. Can't get out of it," she said, taking a sip of champagne. "It's bound to be some party. I heard the pre-sales are the biggest in years for a football book. They expect it to be bigger than Beckham's. Your publisher will have money to burn. There are bound to be some big names around tonight."

"Oh, please don't say that," Alex protested. "I feel nervous enough as it is."

"There's are players and managers going from Liverpool and Manchester," she continued undeterred. "Soap stars, musicians, athletes. Ethan Bower, Rory Evans, Moses Adebayo... They're all going."

Alex froze, backtracking on what she had just said — one name in particular.

"Ethan Bower?" he said. "He's going?"

"Sure. All of them are."

Naz grinned at Alex across the table. "Doesn't he, like, hate you?"

Alex grimaced. "I have no idea."

Naz laughed. "I think you do."

"What's this?" Lanita perked up, a huge smile on her face as she put down her glass. "What have I missed?"

"Nothing," Alex said.

"Alex and Ethan Bower have history," Naz chuckled.

Lanita turned to Alex, her pretty eyes sparkling. "OMG. You haven't shagged him, have you? Tell me you didn't."

"I didn't," he protested. "It's nothing like that."

She groaned. "Pity. Then what? Come on. Spill the story? And how come I don't know this already?"

"It's no big secret," Alex said, shooting Naz a dirty look. "I ghostwrote Ethan's autobiography, which came out about eight years ago."

"You did? I don't even remember him having a book out."

"With good reason. It was a busy time with a lot of big-name biographies vying for the Christmas market. His book kind of got lost in the crowd. It didn't really bother me. As a ghostwriter, they paid me a flat fee. Whether the book was a success or bombed, I got paid just the same."

"So, what's the big deal? Does he think it's your fault his book flopped? I mean, how old was he, anyway? In his twenties? He can't have had much of a story to tell at that age."

Naz cleared his throat theatrically and read aloud from the screen of his phone. "Quote... *'The man who wrote my book didn't do his research and was poorly informed. He seemed like a nice enough guy when we sat down for the interviews, but when he wrote it up, he did a real hatchet job on me. What's written in that book are not my words. He made it up so I would sound like a shallow, egotistical arsehole. I tried to get him fired and hire someone new, but it was too late. The book had to be in the shops by a certain date, and there just wasn't time to start over. I'm glad it didn't do well in the end, so less people got to read that bullshit. Jesus, that guy was a prick.'* End quote." Naz put down the phone, his eyes twinkling with mischief.

"A hatchet job," Lanita said. "Classy."

Alex sighed and swallowed some champagne. It tasted bitter all of a sudden. "That's Ethan's version of what happened."

"And how does your version differ?" she asked. "Dramatically, no doubt."

"The part about him being a shallow, egotistical arsehole... I didn't make that up. It was all there to begin with. All I did was put his personality on the page."

"I've always found him quite charming," she said.

"You know him?"

"A little. Not so much from his competition days, but I've met him recently. In fact, I saw him just last month on a breakfast show, and he was very nice. I wouldn't call him an arsehole at all."

"Maybe he's mellowed. I met him at the height of his success."

Ethan Bower was one of the UK's most triumphant sprinters. He'd won silver and gold medals at both the 2012 and 2016 Olympic Games for the four-hundred-metre races, as well as sharing team glory in the relays. With his wholesome good looks and dazzling green eyes, Ethan had been the poster boy for British athletics when Alex had been approached to pen his biography.

Alex had leapt at the opportunity. Ethan had been one of the UK's most exciting stars...a hero.

Ethan had proved to Alex that the adage of never meeting your heroes was true. With reddish-blond hair, Ethan had the fiery temper to match. As Alex spent time with him for the purpose of the book, he'd witnessed first-hand Ethan's obnoxious behaviour. He'd treated everyone as if they were beneath him — his coach, trainers, physios, ground attendants, reporters and even his fans. He'd been mean-spirited and aggressive and focused on nothing other than his own achievements. His apparent lack of empathy or understanding of others had caused Alex to question more than once whether or not Ethan was a psychopath.

Alex had raised his concerns with the publisher at the time — that he didn't think he could present an impartial view of Ethan, after everything he'd witnessed. They had dismissed his unease. They needed the book in a hurry and didn't care how it was written. Ethan already had a reputation as a bad boy of athletics. No one wanted to read a sanitized version of his story.

"*Throw it all in,*" his editor had advised.

The experience of writing the book had almost put Alex off ghostwriting for life.

Thankfully, none of his other subjects had turned out to be as difficult as Ethan.

"He's pretty hot," Lanita said. "He was always a good-looking guy, but have you seen him recently? OMG, time has been very kind. He's unbelievably fine."

"It doesn't matter what he looks like," Alex said. "It's what's on the inside that counts, and from what I saw, the inside of that man is the worst kind of brat."

"You might be surprised. What you're describing does not sound like the man I know. He was charming, well-spoken...quite humble, in fact."

Alex spluttered, almost choking on his drink. "Humble? Ethan Bower? You have definitely got the wrong guy—not unless he's had a personality transplant. 'Toxic' is the best word I can think of to describe him."

She shrugged. "Well, like I said earlier, it's going to be a big party. You probably won't even see him if he's there. Don't let it spoil your night. It's about you and Fernando, not Ethan."

"Too right," he said. "And if I do see him, you can be sure I'll give him a wide berth. He doesn't like me, and I don't like him. I don't think we have anything to achieve in speaking to each other."

About the Author

Thom Collins is the author of Closer by Morning, with Pride Publishing. His love of page turning thrillers began at an early age when his mother caught him reading the latest Jackie Collins book and promptly confiscated it, sparking a life-long love of raunchy novels.

Thom has lived in the North East of England his whole life. He grew up in Northumberland and now lives in County Durham with his husband and two cats. He loves all kinds of genre fiction, especially bonkbusters, thrillers, romance and horror. He is also a cookery book addict with far too many titles cluttering his shelves. When not writing he can be found in the kitchen trying out new recipes. He's a keen traveler but with a fear of flying that gets worse with age, but since taking his first cruise in 2013 he realized that sailing is the way to go.

Thom loves to hear from readers. You can find his contact information, website details and author profile page at https://www.pride-publishing.com

PUBLISHING

Sign up for our newsletter and find out about all our romance book releases, eBook sales and promotions, sneak peeks and FREE romance books!